The alarm was louder inside the building. Its shriek blared through his head and lodged somewhere in the fillings of his back teeth. He took the hall leading to the office where he'd last spotted Megan.

If an intruder had set off the alarm, he had no time to lose. Police would arrive eventually, but with the weather, he couldn't be sure how soon.

He checked around the corner before stepping into the next hall. What he wouldn't give to have his gun. Armed with only a tire iron, he didn't relish running into whomever set off the alarm. The tool was heavy enough to do some damage, but even so, it would be worthless against even a twenty-two. He had to find Megan. He had to get her the hell out of here.

ANN VOSS PETERSON

A COP IN HER STOCKING

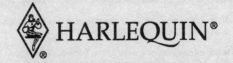

HARLEQUIN®

TORONTO • NEW YORK • LONDON
AMSTERDAM • PARIS • SYDNEY • HAMBURG
STOCKHOLM • ATHENS • TOKYO • MILAN • MADRID
PRAGUE • WARSAW • BUDAPEST • AUCKLAND

To Officer Greg Dixon
and the Middleton Police Department
with special thanks for all you do.

Recycling programs
for this product may
not exist in your area.

ISBN-13: 978-0-373-69505-8

A COP IN HER STOCKING

www.eHarlequin.com

Printed in U.S.A.

ABOUT THE AUTHOR

Ever since she was a little girl making her own books out of construction paper, Ann Voss Peterson wanted to write. So when it came time to choose a major at the University of Wisconsin, creative writing was her only choice. Of course, writing wasn't a *practical* choice—one needs to earn a living. So Ann found jobs, including proofreading legal transcripts, working with quarter horses and washing windows. But no matter how she earned her paycheck, she continued to write the type of stories that captured her heart and imagination—romantic suspense. Ann lives near Madison, Wisconsin, with her husband, her two young sons, her border collie and her quarter horse mare. Ann loves to hear from readers. E-mail her at ann@annvosspeterson.com or visit her Web site at www.annvosspeterson.com.

Books by Ann Voss Peterson

*Wedding Mission

CAST OF CHARACTERS

Tyler Davis—When his old flame returns to town, small-town cop Ty Davis offers to take her son on a Shop with a Cop outing, hoping to give her and her child a merry Christmas. But when the boy disappears in the mall, Ty needs a Christmas miracle of his own.

Megan Garvey—After weathering scandal and divorce, Megan has learned nothing is as it seems. But Ty's loyalty and determination to help her make her want to believe in Santa Claus.

Connor Burke—The three-year-old disappeared in the shopping mall. Will he be home for Christmas?

Doug Burke—Megan's ex-husband is always looking for the easy way out. But when his son goes missing, nothing is easy.

Leo Wheeling—The lieutenant is efficient and on top of things, so why are there so many loose ends in this case?

Todd Baker—The detective has a family of his own, so surely he'll do whatever he can to find Megan's son.

Derek Ernst—The security guard knows all about finding lost children.

Evan Blankenship—The small-town mayor is very helpful. But are his motives rooted in politics or in a secret desire for Megan?

Mr. Keating—The owner of a local security company holds the keys to a lot of doors.

Gary Burke—Is Doug's cousin trying to help Megan out or make things more difficult for her?

Samantha Vickery—What is the woman after?

Chapter One

Try as he might, Tyler Davis was not what anyone would call an expert gift shopper. And if anyone on this snow-covered earth needed proof, here it was, wrapped up in Christmas paper and tied with a big-ass bow.

He tried to tune out the jangle of department store Christmas music and warring scents from the army of perfume pushers and focus on the pair of oversized slippers that resembled a dog's paws clutched in the three-year-old's hands. Even with his deep-seated shopping deficiency, Ty had doubts whether this was the way to go. "You're sure she's going to like those?"

Connor nodded, his tousled red hair flopping over one side of his forehead.

Ty raked his hand through his own cropped, spiky hair. If this was any other kid he'd taken Christmas shopping as part of his small city police department's Shop with a Cop program, he'd find the choice funny. He might even encourage the kid, just for a chuckle. But Megan had been through a lot. And the whole reason he insisted on taking Connor out shopping—secretly on his own dime, since the department's official Shop with a Cop program was already over—was to give Megan a good experience for a change. "I don't know, Connor. Moms usually like things that make them look...I don't know...pretty. Not like a dog."

The inside corners of Connor's eyes reddened. His lips pulled together into what was fast becoming a pout and could any minute cross the line into crying.

Oh, hell.

He must be out of his mind to take his old flame's son shopping. And when he thought about the world of hurt he'd be in if the chief found out he had misrepresented this as an official department program, he knew he'd crossed to the far side of crazy. It was just that when he'd heard how Meg's ex had dragged her through the shredder and seen the dumpy apartment the smartest girl in his high school class was now living in, he'd wanted to do something for her. She couldn't afford a nice Christmas for herself and her young son, but he could. And she never had to know where the money came from.

And besides, it gave him an excuse to see her again.

Of course, he hadn't considered that the success of his brilliant plan all hinged on a three-year-old's taste.

He pulled in a deep breath of patience and let it out slowly. The last thing he wanted was to make the kid cry. Now *that* would really impress Megan, returning with a tear-sodden little boy who could tell her all about what a jerk Officer Ty was. Not that she didn't know that already.

He picked up the slippers and pretended to examine them, turning them over in his hands. "Oh, look here. They're slippers. I didn't realize that. Well, that changes everything. You're right, man. Your mom will love these." He eyed the kid, hoping Connor wouldn't pick up a false note in his voice.

Big green eyes flicked up to his face. A twitch settled over the little lips, not exactly a smile, but something less than a pout.

Crisis mitigated.

Ty handed the fuzzy things back to Connor along with a grin. So Megan would be wearing dog paw slippers this winter. Interesting. "What next? Can you think of something else your mom might like?"

Connor shook his head.

"Should we look around?" His arms were already weighed down with Legos, books and a Hot Wheels set for the kid. But he couldn't leave the mall with nothing but a pair of dog slippers for Megan. He had to find something nice.

He did a 360, gaze skimming over the clothing racks and colorful Christmas displays in the mall department store. His eyes fixed on racks of lacy bras and thongs in the lingerie department nearby.

Hmm. Now he could much more easily picture Megan wearing something in satin or lace. If he hadn't given up his right to play Santa—officially—that's what she would find in her stocking come Christmas morning.

He stepped a little closer. Images of Christmases— back when they were dating in high school and college— danced through his mind like some kind of damn sugar plums. He could imagine what it would be like now. A quiet Christmas Eve, sitting in front of the fire running his fingers through Megan's silky auburn hair. He'd choose something like that black number with the lace that was cut down to there. Or maybe the teddy on the mannequin, green to go with her eyes. Yeah, that was the one. He could imagine her filling it out.

And right after that, he could imagine taking it off.

He shook his head, trying to remove the thought, but he had little luck with that. Seeing her this morning when he'd picked up Connor had been like the return of a delicious dream after five sleepless years. She'd been nervous about taking him up on the shopping offer, he could tell, even without knowing the money was actually coming from him. But when Connor had started jabbering about reindeer and presents and stockings filled to bursting on Christmas morning, the loving smile that had transformed her face had left Ty feeling like Santa himself.

After that, he hadn't stood a chance.

The cloying clash of perfumes in the department store had only reminded him of how good and pure she'd always smelled. The taste of the soft pretzel he'd forced on Connor in the food court had only made him think of how often he and Megan had pooled their change to buy one at the convenience store after school. And each memory brought back thoughts of the cold lump that had formed in his gut when he'd come home from the police academy one weekend and learned she was planning to marry—of all people—Doug Burke.

Oh, hell.

He had to get his focus back on shopping. He was with her kid, for God's sake. He needed to focus on taking

Connor "Shopping with a Cop," not on his personal history with the boy's mother.

Getting the hell away from the lingerie section would be a good first step.

"Let me guess, you're looking for a gift for someone."

The voice came from over his left shoulder. He glanced down to see a woman wearing too much eyeliner smiling at him as if he was the most fascinating man in the world.

He didn't buy it. "Thanks, but I need to get back—"

"It's not a problem. My friends call me the Giftinator." She giggled, the bubbly sound more suitable coming from a fifteen-year-old girl than a grown woman. "Get it? Like *The Terminator?*"

"Funny." He forced a smile. In other circumstances, he might have a little fun joking around, maybe even flirting. But today, it didn't feel…right. "I hate to be rude, but I—"

"Then don't be. Let me help. I'm seriously good at the whole Christmas present thing. I should get a job in a store. Or maybe start my own business as a personal shopper. Not that I could do something like that in a town with only one decent mall. But I really think shopping is my true calling."

Rude or not, Ty glanced back toward the pajamas, stockings and fuzzy footwear. Dog-paw slippers lay on the waxed tile floor. A woman pored over a rack of flannel drawstring pants. A tinny version of "Silver Bells" tinkled in the air.

Great. He'd only been ten or fifteen feet from Connor,

but that was enough for the boy to feel like he could wander away. Ty couldn't blame him. He'd probably gotten bored waiting for Ty to quit talking…well, listening would be more accurate.

He gave the woman a cursory glance and a mumbled *excuse me,* and strode back to the slipper rack. "Connor?" His gaze landed on a family of four over in the shoe department, an older couple shopping for jewelry and a woman parked at the makeup counter wearing a sweater covered in Christmas trees. No little boy with tousled red hair.

His breath stuttered in his chest. "Connor?"

Nothing.

He bolted across the aisle and circled the rack of slippers. The kid had to be here somewhere. Didn't he?

The aisle behind the rack was vacant.

"Connor?" He let his voice boom this time. Maybe he was off looking at something for Megan, or playing with another kid. Ty did another scan of the store. The woman who had tried to monopolize his attention was gone. He spotted nothing but lingerie, women's pajamas and formal dresses tucked far in the corner.

"Did you lose someone?" The woman absorbed in flannel pj's gave him a sympathetic, if slightly amused, smile.

Ty was not finding this amusing in the least. "Little boy. Three years old. Red hair. Have you seen him?"

"No. But maybe he's hiding in one of those circular clothing racks. My kids always liked to do that at a certain age."

Hiding. Great. Ty strode to the pajamas and peered

inside the ring of clothing. Nothing. He moved from rack to rack; all of them in the area were empty. "Connor? Connor Burke? You need to come out *right now*."

Nothing. No answer. No movement. No boy.

He grabbed for his cell phone and flagged down a store employee. It was time to call for backup. Store security, shoppers, the entire Lake Hubbard police department, the damn FBI. Whatever it took. He had to find Connor, and he had to find him now.

Chapter Two

The cramped little office tucked into a corner of the department store's upper level smelled sharp with body odor and stress. Ty could only guess that most of it was coming from him, but the mall security guy hunching over the computer that collected the feeds from the store's security cameras seemed awfully fragrant, as well.

Ty jammed in beside his lieutenant, Leo Wheeling, and held his breath while the security dude flipped through each of the store's video cameras. "Can't tell you how many kids I help track down every month."

"That so?" Leo said, focused on the screen. "You work a lot…"

"Derek."

"You working a lot lately, Derek?"

"Sure am. This time of year is even busier than tourist season. Just this weekend, in fact, I returned two different kids to their mothers." He puffed out his polyester-clad chest just a little and pushed his glasses back up his nose. "This one? He probably just ran off. They usually do. Get bored or whatnot and want to find some toys to look at."

"Sounds like you have a lot of experience." Leo sounded a bit bored and whatnot himself, yet somehow he still managed to be polite.

At this point, Ty had sworn off politeness for the rest of his life. He just wanted the guy to shut the hell up. He was about to share that sentiment when the lingerie department flashed on the screen. "That's it. That's the camera. That's where I last saw Connor."

Leo glanced at him, his bushy blond eyebrows pulling low. "You took the kid shopping for bras?"

"Slippers." Ty pointed to the image of the slipper rack beyond the lacy under things. "He wanted to buy his mom dog paw slippers."

The security man squinted up at him through coke-bottle lenses. "How long you want to go back?"

Ty glanced at his watch. "Almost a half hour." He couldn't believe that much time had already passed. They had locked down the store right away. But even though patrol officers and store security personnel were all combing the area, they hadn't found a single sign of Connor. In those precious minutes that Ty was being polite to a stranger, Connor had seemingly vanished. He prayed the video would give them an idea of where the boy had gone.

He forced himself to concentrate on the speeding images moving in reverse on the screen, not on what might have happened to Megan's son. He spotted himself, racing around the area backward, peeking in the circular clothing racks, talking to the woman holding flannel. And there he was, peering at the lingerie, listening politely to the woman who called herself the Giftinator, barely visible on the screen. And then...

The angle wasn't great, the camera was too far from the slipper rack to show much detail, but what he did see sent a chill down his spine. A man in a shapeless coat and hood. Then the man was gone, and Connor was there, clutching those dog paw slippers. "That's it. Stop."

The security tech stopped the reversing images.

"Okay. Play it."

Ty held his breath and watched as the action went forward at normal speed. Him talking to Connor. Him drifting a few feet away to the lingerie, leaving the poor kid all alone. The figure in the shapeless coat stepping around the slipper rack, taking Connor's hand and leading him to the exit nearby.

"Fifteen feet away. I was only fifteen feet away." Yet he'd been so caught up in his memories of Megan, in his selfish fantasies, in being polite to that woman, he hadn't even noticed the man in the parka. He hadn't had a clue that Connor was gone.

Not until it was too late.

Leo leaned over the security system tech's shoulder. "Can you save that section of the recording and get me images from the camera for that exit?" He pointed toward the one where the man in the parka and Connor had disappeared.

"Sure thing."

"After you're done with that, check prior footage for all the exits, starting with that one. He must have entered the store at some point. I want a face shot of him. Anything we can use to get an ID."

The tech nodded and started tapping keys.

The lieutenant turned his laser gaze on Ty. "You know the ex-husband. Could this be him?"

Ty considered for a moment. "Hard to tell without a better view of his face. But the body type fits." Or at least as much of it as he could see in the oversized parka.

Leo nodded. "Average height, average weight?"

"Like most of the male population."

"It's something. We need to have the mother take a look at whatever pictures we can get of this guy. Even if he isn't the ex, she might know him. There's a chance."

A cramp seized Ty's chest. He knew the odds of an abducted kid being found, and they weren't good, especially if the abductor was a stranger. Either it happened right away, in the first forty-eight hours, or it wasn't likely to end well.

This was his fault. All his fault.

Leo let out a sigh and clapped the security guy on the shoulder. "The moment you find any kind of a face shot, let me know."

"I sure will."

"I'm calling the feds' CARD team to give them a heads-up. I want to be prepared, and if this isn't the ex, we could use the help. And we need to be ready to issue an Amber Alert."

Ty nodded. CARD stood for Child Abduction Rapid Deployment, one of ten teams of experts located across the nation. Each team member had extensive experience in crimes-against-children investigations, particularly cases where the abductor was not a family member, and Ty was glad to hear Leo wasn't planning to mess around.

The Lake Hubbard P.D. was awfully small to handle a case like this on their own. Even with help from the sheriff's department, it would be nice to have the extra resources. "What do you want me to do?"

"Sorry, Ty. I want you to lay back a little on this. At least until I get the word on how the chief wants to proceed."

Ty knew there would be consequences to pretending his shopping trip was an official police department program. On top of that, when the media found out about him losing Connor, the blowback would only get worse. But whatever happened, he didn't care. All he could think about was that little boy. "You'll need photos of Connor for the search and Amber Alert."

"I'll send Baker to notify the child's mother and have her take a look at the images of this guy. He can ask her for pictures."

Nothing against Baker. He was a good cop. But it wasn't right that Megan hear about this from a stranger. "Can I do it?"

Leo gave him a frown, lines digging into his forehead, deep as trenches.

"You got to let me do it, Leo."

"You really want to?"

Of course, he didn't. Not one bit. "I have to."

"All right. Go with Baker."

"Thanks. I couldn't live with myself if she heard it from someone other than me." Truth was, he wasn't sure he could live with himself even now.

WHEN THE DOOR BUZZER SOUNDED and Megan glanced out the window, she was expecting to see a police car in front of her building. She wasn't ready for the tremor that seized her stomach and made her head swirl like she'd just climbed off a carnival ride.

It was so strange, seeing Ty again after all these years.

She pushed her hair back from her face and ran her fingers through the ends. Man, she was pitiful, but she couldn't help it. She'd even put makeup on this morning before he'd stopped by to pick up her son. Not because she hoped for something between them. Any hope of that had fizzled out years ago, during that awful summer and in the fall afterward when Ty had left to attend a police academy in Madison.

Not that it mattered. She'd done marriage, and there wasn't a chance she was gullible enough to try it again. But there was just something about the way Ty looked at her that made her want to show him the fabulous woman he'd lost all those years ago. Rub his face in it a bit. Silly, vain, and more than a little vengeful, she admitted, but there it was.

Much more important than old feelings between her and Ty was whether the shopping trip with Connor had gone well.

A stronger jitter gripped her stomach and climbed into her chest. Her little guy had been through so much with the divorce. And now that they'd left Chicago and moved back across the Wisconsin border to Lake Hubbard, she could tell he missed his dad. That was the reason she'd let Ty talk her into taking him on this outing when he'd told her there were leftover donations to the Shop with a Cop program. Connor needed some time with a man, and that was something she couldn't provide. And this morning he'd been so excited…it was almost as if the opportunity was tailor-made.

But that didn't mean she wasn't nervous about it. She was nervous every time Connor was out of her sight. At least today he was with a police officer. She just hoped his experience was a positive one.

The outside buzzer blared again through her apartment.

Running her fingers through her hair a couple more times, she crossed the living room and hit the button unlocking the building's main door, a low buzz humming through the halls.

She couldn't wait to see Connor's face. Please, let him be happy. She opened her apartment door and stepped out into the long corridor.

A man's steps thunked up the stairs and echoed in the open stairwell and lobby below.

Leaving her door ajar, Megan started down the hall, hurriedly padding on stocking feet to meet the sound, eager to see her son's face.

A blue-clad leg and black shoe crested the top step. Ty Davis stepped around the corner and into the hall.

She focused on Ty's face, and for a moment, her heart felt like it fluttered, just like it had when she'd first laid eyes on him back in high school. Then it occurred to her that he didn't look happy.

She glanced down the staircase. A cop in full uniform climbed the staircase behind him but no little boy. She hurried toward Ty. "Where's Connor?"

His face appeared tighter the closer she came. Lines

etched his forehead and cupped around the corners of his lips.

"Where's Connor?" she repeated. Hadn't he heard her? What was wrong with him? "Is he hurt?"

"We need to talk, Meg." He cupped a hand under her elbow and steered her away from the stairs. "Let's go back inside your apartment for a moment."

Her breath seemed to clog her throat. Something had happened. That much was clear.

"Meg?"

Now was not the time to lose her head. She couldn't let her mind race off in a panic…not until she knew what it was she faced. "Oh…okay."

Without releasing her, he moved her hand into the crook of his arm and guided her back to her open door.

Possibilities whipped through her mind. Was Connor hurt? Had he tried to steal something? Had her mother wandered off from the nursing home? Or had she died, and Ty hadn't wanted Connor here when he broke the news? She moved one foot in front of the other, reaching the apartment, stepping inside. She stopped and angled her body to face Ty. Her hands were shaking and she gripped them together to keep them still. "What happened?"

"I think you should sit down."

Sit down? Like hell. "What happened?" Panic shrieked inside her, but her voice became quieter the louder her fear.

He paused, searching for words or still waiting for her to take a seat, she didn't know.

Clearly something had happened. Something she hadn't

seen coming. Something she'd missed. "Tell me, Ty. Please."

He gave a slow nod. "I'm so sorry, Megan."

Her lungs contracted. She couldn't breathe. "My mother?"

"It's Connor. He was abducted from the store."

She shook her head. It didn't make sense. "But he was with you."

He flinched ever so slightly, as if the statement caused him pain. "The entire department is looking for him. Store security, too. We'll find him, Megan. We're going to find him."

"No. No." She couldn't stop shaking her head. She hadn't seen this coming, all right. She hadn't seen it, because it was impossible. "He was with you. This can't happen."

"I'm so sorry."

She swayed. Her knees felt like they were going to buckle, but she willed herself to stand on her own. This couldn't be happening. There had to be some kind of explanation. Some kind of sick joke. She waited for him to tell her that he was kidding, to take it all back, to… something, but she knew deep inside that something wasn't going to come.

Her baby was gone.

Chapter Three

Ty didn't know how much Megan was absorbing. She stared at him, green eyes wide and a little glassy. And although she nodded at the appropriate times, there was a blankness to her expression that felt hard and brittle at the same time, like the face of a porcelain doll.

"Doug."

"Officers are trying to reach him."

"Could he...could he have taken Connor?"

"We're looking into it. Believe me." Ty wanted to go question the bastard himself, but the lieutenant wouldn't allow it. Probably a good idea. If Doug did sneak Connor out of the store under Ty's nose, Ty wasn't sure he could leave the interview without beating the tar out of him.

Still, compared to the alternative, Doug being the kidnapper would be a huge relief. "You can help us determine if Doug took him."

"How?"

He motioned to Baker. Even though the detective was supposed to be in charge of this notification and interview, he'd hung back and let Ty take the reins. Todd Baker was a good guy.

Baker set up his laptop on the coffee table and recalled the pictures they had downloaded from the security footage. The first image of the kidnapper came on the screen, a shot of the parka-clad man approaching Connor. Ty was also visible just a few feet away.

Megan gasped.

"You recognize him?"

She shook her head. "No. Not really. I mean, it could be Doug, but…" Her eyebrows pulled low over worried eyes. Her chin trembled. "I can't really tell."

"We have a few different angles." Ty glanced at Baker.

He rolled the snips of video and magnified the kidnapper. "Better?"

Megan shook her head. Tears wound down her cheeks, but she didn't make a sound.

Baker stopped the video on an image. A sliver of the kidnapper's cheek peeked from beneath the hood. "That's as good a shot of his face as we could come up with."

It was strange, Ty had to admit. In each bit of video, the kidnapper had averted his face at just the right angle and pulled up his hood in just the right amount to avoid security cameras.

Megan shook her head. "I don't know. It could be Doug. It also could be almost anyone."

Ty stared at the image, comparing it to his memories of Doug Burke's face. She was right. It could be almost anyone.

"You lost him…how did you lose him? You're right there." Her voice was only a whisper, yet it cut into him like a whip crack.

He met her eyes. They glistened in the muted light of the window. A few tears spiked her lashes and escaped down her cheeks.

He could understand her frustration, understand her fear. Scratch that. He couldn't truly understand. But he could imagine it. And if he were in her place right now, he imagined he would be furious. One thing was certain. He more than deserved her fury. "I'm so sorry, Meg."

She didn't answer. She looked back at the image on the computer.

"The department is working on finding him," Baker said in a steady voice. "We are searching every inch of the mall. We've contacted the FBI, in case we need their help. We are prepared to issue an Amber Alert. Everyone is on this."

Ty had already told her all this, but he was grateful for Baker's calm, reliable recitation. Maybe Leo was right. Maybe Baker should have broken the news to Megan instead of him. He had a steady influence Ty couldn't come close to matching. But the thought of not being there when Megan needed him wasn't acceptable. Not again.

"How did it happen? What were you thinking? What were you doing that you weren't watching him?" She hadn't looked up, but it was clear she was talking to him.

He opened his mouth, then shut it tight. What could he say? That he was looking at lingerie? That he was fantasizing about how she'd look in it? Imagining taking it off her? "I was…shopping. I only took my eye off him for a moment." He decided not to mention the Giftinator.

Megan would only think he'd been flirting instead of paying attention to her son. It hadn't been like that, not at all. But he wouldn't be able to convince her.

Not that it mattered. He'd been absorbed in his own world, his own concerns. He hadn't been focused on her son. He deserved all the blame she could heap on him.

"A moment..." She buried her face in her hands. Her shoulders jerked, a silent sob shuddering through her body.

He wanted to touch her, soothe her, promise it would be okay. But he doubted she would accept his touch, and right now even he had trouble believing that promise.

"I want to go to the mall. I have to go to the mall." She pushed herself up from her chair. "I need to find him."

He stood and reached out. But instead of grasping her arm, he let his hand hover in the air.

Baker stood, as well. "We have officers all over the store. People from our department. From the sheriff's department. Store security. They are professionals. Let them handle this."

She shook her head. For a moment, Ty thought she might bolt for the door, then she focused on him. Her eyes shifted back and forth as if she didn't know where to look.

If Ty knew anything about Megan, even after all these years, it was that she was not good at accepting anything from anyone. Not help, not reassurance, not promises—regardless of whether those promises were likely to be kept. But she was comfortable doing. "There's nothing you can do there that they can't. But here, there's a lot only you can do here."

"Only me...like what?"

"First, you need to stay by the phone."

"You think there might be a phone call? Like a ransom call?"

"Maybe. Or someone might find Connor or see him and give you a call. You need to be here to answer."

She stared past him, focusing on the twinkle lights and colorful jumble of decorations covering her Christmas tree, her eyes unseeing, her expression blank.

"There's more, more you can do."

She returned her gaze to his.

"We need recent pictures of Connor to release to the media and use in the search. Can you compile some?"

"Of course." Taking a deep breath, she turned away from him and half ran toward the bedroom. A few moments later, she came back with a wad of photos cradled in her hands. "I have a lot of them. I printed them out to make a collage for my mom as a Christmas present."

She shuffled through the stack of pictures as if they were playing cards. "School pictures, some from his birthday, Halloween. No. What am I thinking? He's in a costume on Halloween. That's not going to help." Except for a few stray tears, she hadn't cried since he'd broken the news, but now tears swamped her eyes and gushed down her cheeks.

"I'm so sorry, Meg," he said again. He could never say it enough. He took a chance and grabbed hold of her hand.

Her throat moved as if she was swallowing emotion, preventing it from further breaking free. Finally she looked him in the eye. "I know you didn't mean to lose him. I've had him wander off when I was shopping with him, too."

The fact that she would think about reassuring him in the midst of all she was facing made him feel worse than he already did. He rubbed his hand up her arm, as if simple friction would warm the chill that he knew was running through her. "We'll find him. We'll get him back to you."

"I should have told him to stay next to you in the store, to hold your hand. I should have known something like this could happen. I meant to remind him to stay close to you before he left, but it slipped my mind. God, I'm so stupid."

He couldn't stand this. "No. *I'm* stupid. *I* wasn't paying attention. *I* lost Connor."

She shook her head, but the tears didn't stop flowing. She pushed the photos into his hands. "Here. I'll see if I can find any better ones."

He set the pictures on the table and took both her hands in his. He looked down into her wet green eyes, eyes that were so desperate. "I will find Connor. I will make all of this okay. I promise."

Maybe an impossible vow. But God help him, he had never meant anything more.

MEGAN WAS EXHAUSTED, frustrated and more than a little panicky by the time Ty's lieutenant arrived at the apartment to fill her in on the search and ask her to repeat everything she'd already discussed with Ty. At Ty's direction, she'd written a detailed description of her son and everything he'd been wearing down to the

Hot Wheels sneakers on his feet. She'd also compiled a list of names, addresses and phone numbers of family, friends, babysitters, anyone she could think of who had come in contact with Connor, both in Lake Hubbard and Chicago.

Ty had made copies of all the photos she'd dug up, ready to send them to every law enforcement agency in the vicinity and nonprofit organization that helped find missing children.

She knew Ty would be helping her find Connor even if he didn't feel guilty about his role in losing him. He was a police officer, after all. This kind of thing was his job. And more than that, it was the kind of person Ty was, the kind he'd been raised to be.

But although she felt plenty angry that he'd lost her son, she couldn't see what good anger and blame would do. Not now. There wasn't time. All she could focus on right now was getting her son back, and she badly needed to trust that Ty and the Lake Hubbard police department could help her do that.

"Ms. Garvey?" Ty's lieutenant perched on the edge of a chair and leveled her with an officious look. "With your permission, we would like to put a trap and trace on your phone."

Lieutenant Leo Wheeling had to be the squarest man she'd ever met. His attitude, his blocky chest and short legs, his cropped blond hair and carefully trimmed mustache, everything about the man was right angles. And although she'd learned from experience not to rely on anyone but herself, the sheer regular nature of the guy made her want to trust he'd come through. "You think the kidnapper will call?"

"We hope he will."

"To ask for ransom?"

"Yes."

She motioned to the shabby little apartment, the cheap Christmas tree she'd bought in a discount lot, already dropping needles. The decorations made of paper and pipe cleaners and good old-fashioned popcorn on strings she'd used to round out the few good decorations she had left from the house in Chicago. Not to mention the sparse secondhand furniture underneath it all, a veritable museum of particle board and pilled cushions. "I obviously have no money. What could he want that I could give him?"

"We don't know, Ms. Garvey. We are trying to cover all the bases."

She nodded. She should be glad of that, not giving the man a hard time.

A knock sounded at the door. Ty opened it. A familiar-looking man dressed in a suit and dark overcoat pushed into the room and focused on her. "Megan. I came when I heard." He thrust out his hand and grasped hers, but instead of giving it a shake, he simply held it and stared into her eyes.

He looked so familiar. The sharp nose. The high forehead. "I'm sorry, do I know you?"

"Evan Blankenship. We went to high school together."

Memories shuffled into place in her mind. "Of course. You were a few years older, right?"

"You had to remind me." He chuckled and glanced at the other newcomers over his shoulder, then back to her.

"And I heard you married Dee Dee Harris." Megan almost lapsed into the envious nickname Dee Dee had been given by the other girls in high school, Harris the Heiress, but stopped herself just in time.

"Three years now." Evan held up his ring as if offering proof.

"Lucky man." It seemed ridiculous to be chatting about normal life as if everything was…normal. But somehow just the ordinariness of the exchange made Megan feel a little more grounded.

"Don't I know it. I was also elected mayor of Lake Hubbard in a special election this fall. That's why I stopped by, to offer my support as an elected official and an old friend."

"Uh, thank you."

"And my help. Seriously, Megan, if there's anything Dee Dee and I can do to get your little boy back—connections, money, anything at all—you let me know."

She fished for a way to respond, finally settling on another "Thank you."

"I understand the FBI is on its way?"

Again Megan nodded. She hadn't been sure how to take this outpouring of generosity from a man she hadn't talked to since high school. Even then, he'd been Doug's age, not hers. She'd hardly known him. But after that last comment, she had to wonder if he was here to see the FBI. Maybe Mayor Evan Blankenship had watched too many crime shows on TV and simply wanted to see the bureau in action.

She gave him what she could muster for a smile and excused herself. She didn't like being so cynical, thinking poorly of others' motives, not trusting anyone at their word, but she couldn't help it. The last years had bled her dry of trust and optimism, and the past couple of hours didn't seem likely to change that.

Her throat thickened. Her chest physically hurt with each beat of her heart, and she knew the only thing that would make it stop was clutching Connor close. Standing, she excused herself and walked out of the living room and down the short hall.

She had to get away. Just for a moment. She had to catch her breath. She wanted to be somewhere she could feel closer to her son.

She slipped into Connor's room and pulled in a deep breath. The place smelled of him, of crayons and Lincoln Logs and the orange-flavored candy he'd accidently gotten stuck in a corner of the carpet. She looked around at his toys, at his unmade bed, at his jammies lying in a wadded-up clump on the floor. For a moment, the walls blurred, the Thomas the Tank Engine clock became merely a smudge of bright reds and blues against the white wall.

She tilted her chin back and did her best to blink away tears. They would find him, wouldn't they? She had to trust they'd find him. She didn't know how she'd cope otherwise.

"Meg?"

Her body swayed toward the sound of Ty's voice and

his old nickname for her coming from right behind her. If she turned around, if she reached for him—allowed herself to curl up in his arms, to soak in his comfort, to accept his strength—she knew he'd oblige. He would again promise to find Connor. He'd reassure her that everything would be okay. She wanted those things so badly. She wanted to trust he could provide them.

But she knew things weren't as simple as that. They never were. To get her son back, she needed to be strong. She couldn't rely on anyone else to make things okay. She'd known that most of her life. She couldn't let herself forget it now.

She wiped her cheeks with her fingertips. Pulling in a shuddering breath, she turned around and searched his face, his clear blue eyes, the creases around his mouth, the shadow of stubble beginning to show on his chin. But as much as she wanted to see relief in his eyes and the joy of good news curving his lips, they weren't there.

She braced herself. "Have you gotten hold of Doug?"

"Still no answer."

"You tried the cell number?"

He nodded.

She dropped her focus to the carpet. Large, colorful Duplo Legos scattered the worn Berber. She had the urge to drop to her knees and fit them together, to fit something together, anything. The minute hand on the train clock clicked forward.

How long she stared at those blocks, she wasn't sure, but she heard another tick. Then another. She could feel Ty watching her, but she couldn't bring herself to meet his eyes.

Connor. Out there somewhere. With a stranger.

She felt sick. She felt weak.

She felt angry as hell.

She folded her arms tight across her chest and hung on. "A few years ago, Doug got in some trouble with the law."

Ty's brows arched upward, as if he was surprised, but something in his eyes told her the expression was more acting than truth. Of course she'd be naive to think that the news of Doug's embezzlement and the hell she'd gone through hadn't reached their hometown. Lake Hubbard had grown a lot over the years, but it still had the feel of a small town. And in small towns, gossip traveled fast.

Gossip or not, she was grateful he didn't ask questions. She didn't want to get into the story. Especially with Ty. "He got out of it with a slap on the wrist and swears he's a model citizen now, but he might not be eager to answer a phone call from police."

"I see. Would you be willing to give him a call?"

She nodded. She prayed he had taken Connor. At least then she'd know her little boy was safe. She couldn't rely on Doug for much, but for all his faults, he was truly fond of his son.

"It's worth a shot. I'll let Leo know. We can put your phone on speaker."

"No. I want to make the call alone."

His lips flattened into a line.

"I'll use my cell. Please, Ty. This is all…too much." She gestured to the officers down the hall in the living room. It appeared as though the mayor had left, but the lieutenant, Detective Baker and another detective she didn't know still milled around the Christmas tree.

She didn't want any of them listening in on her call to Doug. Whether Doug had Connor or not, he would blame everything on Ty, chalk up everything to their past relationship, as distant a memory as it was. Doug had always felt threatened by Ty, even though she and Ty had broken up long before. Even though she'd married Doug in the end. Sometimes his comments were very hurtful, and she didn't want them on the speakerphone for all to hear.

Ty finally nodded. "Don't let him upset you. Tell him it was all my fault. After all, it was."

She'd seen the video, and she wasn't so sure of that. Of course he would say the same thing if it wasn't. "If you'll excuse me?"

Ty spun around and headed back down the hall. Her cell phone started ringing before she could get the door closed. She fished it out of her pocket with shaking fingers and flipped it open. "Doug?"

"Get the cops out of your apartment."

Megan shuddered at the low, brutal voice. Not Doug. The kidnapper. It had to be. Somehow he'd gotten the number of her cell phone. And he was watching her apartment.

"Tell them someone you trust has your son."

She wasn't sure she could push a single sound from her throat, but somehow she managed. "Who?" There weren't many people she trusted. And the police had probably checked with everyone she'd put on the list by now.

"A friend. The boy's father. I don't care who. Just convince the police they no longer have to look for your son."

She could hardly breathe.

"Do you want to see your son again?"

"Yes. Okay. I'll get rid of the police."

"Then I want you to go to work tonight."

She couldn't have heard him right. "Work?"

"You do work for Brilliance Cleaning?"

"Yes."

"You are scheduled to clean Keating Security tonight?"

He knew everything about her. "Who is this?"

"That's not your problem. Your problem is that I have your son, and if you don't do everything I say, you won't see him again. At least not alive. Understand?"

A scream built in her throat. She pushed it back. "Yes. I understand."

"While you are cleaning tonight, you will copy their client files off the secure server, including all the specifications of each client's security system. Do you understand?"

"Yes." She understood perfectly. He was asking her to steal sensitive files. Files that could be used to get into any of the security company's clients' businesses and homes undetected. Files that would work like a magic key, allowing him to walk in any of those places he wanted, take anything he wanted and never get caught.

But although she felt a pang of guilt at the idea of stealing the information for him, she wouldn't let it stop her. In the end, it wasn't much of a choice. Connor was the only thing she cared about. She would do anything to get him back. "Then what?"

"I'll tell you after you have the files. Do what I ask, Ms. Garvey. I mean it. Or Santa won't be coming to your house this Christmas."

Chapter Four

"So you'll do it? You'll call the lieutenant and tell him you took Connor from the mall?" Megan held her breath. Doug had reacted to the news just the way she'd thought he would. A lot of blustering about Ty's role, a lot of blaming. But in the end, he'd been just as worried about the ransom call as she was. She just needed to know that he'd hold up his end—she needed to hear him swear it—before she went out to talk to Lieutenant Wheeling.

"And then what happens? I take the blame for this? I get arrested?"

"I'll back you up. I'll tell them it was a misunderstanding, that we've worked everything out." She wasn't sure if that would be enough to protect him, but she hoped it would at least convince him to go along.

"And I'm supposed to stick my neck out and trust you to explain things?"

"I *will* explain things."

"Right. If I had a more devious mind, I might think you and Davis set this up. That he faked the kidnapping so you could trap me with some kind of kidnapping charge and take full custody."

She closed her eyes. She'd only needed Doug to come through for her twice in all their time together, after Connor was born and now. He'd failed her the first time. She had to make sure he came through for her now. "I will make sure you don't get in trouble for this, Doug. I promise. But I need you to do this. Connor needs you to do this. Please."

"I suppose."

She recognized the smug tone in his voice. She could picture him right now in her mind's eye, all inflated and self-important. The strange thing was, she didn't care. She'd tell him anything he wanted to hear, just as long as he came through on his end. The only person she cared about was her son. "Thank you. You'll call him now?"

"Yes."

"You have his phone number?"

"He's called me a dozen times in the past hour, I swear. All I have to do is call him back."

"Thank you."

"I want you to remember this, Megan."

"Don't you worry. I will." She ended the call. She was still shaking, but at least she felt like she had a plan, a plan that was underway.

She'd wait for Doug to make his call, then give the lieutenant all the reassurances he needed from her end. He had no reason not to believe her. It would all go smoothly. It had to.

"Was that Doug?"

Ty's voice jolted along her nerves like an electric shock. She'd been so focused on convincing Doug to call Lieutenant Wheeling and then doing her own explaining that she'd almost forgotten she also had to lie to Ty. "Yes. He promised to call your lieutenant back right away."

Ty nodded. "Does he know anything?"

"Yes. He has Connor. That was him at the mall." She tried to give him a relieved smile, but she wasn't sure she remembered what that felt like. "So everything is okay."

"Really?"

What did that mean? That he didn't buy it? "Yes. He saw you with him at the store, and, well, he got jealous. He called me to let me know everything's okay. Everything's over."

She expected him to look relieved. Something. But his expression didn't change. "You have to tell Lieutenant Wheeling. But I have to warn you everything is not likely to be over instantly."

"What do you mean?"

"We're going to have to investigate what happened. Make sure Connor is okay."

"Why? There's no need for it."

"That's good. I'm glad. But we have to confirm that fact in order to close the investigation."

"But I'm telling you that he's safe."

Ty held up his hands.

Megan's mind raced. If the police went after Doug for the story they'd concocted, he'd tell them the truth for sure. It would all be over. She couldn't let that happen. "You can't do anything if I don't cooperate."

"The department has an obligation to check on Connor's welfare."

"You can't charge Doug with anything for taking his own son."

"If he has Connor and the boy is all right, there shouldn't be any problem."

"So what happens now?"

"We tell Leo. He'll take it from there."

And judging by the squareness of the man, she'd be willing to bet he'd follow procedure to a *T*. Which probably meant she didn't have much time before the police would know Doug didn't have Connor at all. She had to head this off, or at least buy some time until she could give the kidnapper what he wanted and get her son back.

She stepped toward Ty and laid a hand on his arm. "I don't want the police to harass Doug. He's Connor's father. I have to deal with him. Something like this... he'll blame me. He'll make things miserable for me, just because he can."

She wasn't sure if she could convince the lieutenant and the other officers out in her living room, but maybe she could appeal to Ty. He wanted to help her. If she could convince him, maybe he'd convince his lieutenant. "Things are fine between me and Doug right now. I don't want to ruin that balance."

"He took your son without telling you. That doesn't seem fine to me."

"He was upset when he saw I let Connor go shopping with you. I think he felt like you were trying to take his place with his son. But I talked to him. Now he understands that's not true. I also talked to Connor. Everything is fine. Can't this whole thing just be over?"

"It's not that simple, Meg."

"Can we *try* to make it that simple?"

He didn't answer.

Seconds stretched, one after another until Megan thought she might fall to her knees and beg. She couldn't let things unfold this way.

"All right."

Ty's answer was so low, at first Megan thought she might have imagined it. "Did you say yes?"

"I'll talk to Leo."

"Doug said he'd return the Lieutenant's calls."

"Good. He'd better do that. The sooner, the better."

"He will."

Ty stepped toward the hall, then paused. He turned back to face her, lines digging into his forehead and bracketing his mouth. "Who called earlier? Right when I left you?"

Megan had been ready with the story she'd cooked up with Doug, but she wasn't prepared for this. Ty must have heard her cell phone ring as she closed Connor's bedroom door. "It was…it was Doug."

Ty watched her carefully. "That's a coincidence. You were about to call him."

He might have been just making a casual observation, but Megan didn't think so. More likely, he suspected she was lying. A jitter seized her stomach. "A coincidence. Yes, it was. At least everything worked out. Connor is safe, and everything is fine."

"Glad to hear Connor is okay. That's the important part." Again he started to leave, then caught himself. This time when he returned his gaze to hers, his eyes held something softer. Sadder. "I don't understand why you're still protecting Doug."

She wished she could tell him the truth. That this wasn't about protecting Doug at all but protecting Connor. She wished she could trust that if Ty knew the real situation, he would stick by her. But wishing didn't change anything. He was a cop, and she was about to become a criminal. That was the way things were.

It was up to her to get her baby back, to make him safe. She was on her own.

Ty DIDN'T BELIEVE MEGAN'S story. Not for a second. The entire time she'd been talking, her eyelashes had fluttered and her cheeks had flushed a delicate shade of pink. When she'd related the part about how Doug had seen the error of his jealous ways, her eyes had shifted to the side, as if she found something fascinating near his left ear. She was about as good at lying as the teenagers he discovered throwing toilet paper into the trees outside the high school last Halloween.

The thing that had him confused was why.

Had Doug threatened to hurt his own little boy? Told Megan he wouldn't let her see him again if she got him in trouble with police? As much as Ty despised Doug, he couldn't see him hurting his own son. He knew it happened all the time, parents abusing their children, using them as weapons against one another. But Doug? And no matter what Doug would or wouldn't do, Ty could never imagine Megan leaving her son with a man who would threaten him.

He rubbed a hand over his face and walked into her

living room. Somewhere in the back of his mind, the thought of Megan getting back together again with Doug jabbed at him. Stupid. It was none of his business what Megan decided to do with her life. If she was protecting Doug out of some desire to have him return to her and Connor, who was he to say anything about it?

Ty had had his chance. He'd made his choice, just as Megan had made hers. His feelings now had more to do with the self-centered fantasies he'd been entertaining since he'd learned she was back in Lake Hubbard. Fantasies that she'd realized her mistake, that she'd come here for him. Fantasies that he could undo the damage he'd done when he'd left her all those years ago.

Left her just when she needed him most.

When he'd stepped out of the living room to check up on Megan, it had been filled with officers. The mayor had already gone, but Baker and two other guys had stayed, drinking Megan's coffee and waiting for word that someone had seen Connor. Now only Leo remained, standing in the kitchenette, a cell phone to his ear. A few overheard words, and Ty knew why the others had gone.

"You understand I'm going to walk in the next room and check with her on all this right now." A pause stretched as Ty imagined Doug explaining.

Ty turned away. So Doug had come through on his promise. Megan should be happy to know that her faith in him was rewarded. And when Leo got off the phone, Ty would put in a few words, just as he'd promised.

Whether he liked it or not, the rest was none of his business.

Ty contented himself with staring at the cute little tree Megan had decorated and listened to the hum of Leo's even voice. The decorations, the apartment, it was all so Megan. Nothing fancy, but everything well thought out, designed all on her own, and nearly pulsing with love. It reminded him of Christmases back when he was a kid. More holiday joy than presents. His dad doting on him. And he and his school-teacher mom spending every day of their long school breaks doing something fun.

Finally the lieutenant clapped his phone shut and glanced up at him. "You've heard?"

Ty pulled his gaze from a construction paper cutout of a three-year-old's interpretation of Santa Claus and faced his lieutenant. "Megan told me. So what's going to happen to good old Doug?"

"Not sure yet. But if Ms. Garvey is as okay with it as Burke seems to think, we're not inclined to pursue this. I'll have to talk to the chief, of course. But custody situations are sticky at best, and if neither one has a problem, I sure don't. We'll cross our t's and dot our i's, of course. Check up on the child. But we don't have the manpower to spend a lot of time on something that seems to be resolved."

What could he say? He already knew how Megan would answer Leo's questions. He arched his brows. "I noticed the place cleared out pretty quickly."

Leo frowned and looked past Ty and out the window. "Big accident on County H. And the snow has just started."

"Do they need extra help?" Apparently Megan didn't

need him here. At least if he could help with the storm they were supposed to get tonight, he'd feel useful.

Leo leveled him with a serious look. "We need to talk."

Ty didn't like the sound of that. He waited for Leo to go on, not wanting to encourage him.

The lieutenant rubbed his chin, the chaffing sound of stubble giving away the lateness of the hour. "I talked to the chief."

Ty braced himself. "And?"

"We're putting you on suspension, Ty, and we're going to investigate exactly what happened today."

The news clanged in his ears. "So I'm going to be investigated, and Burke is in the clear. The justice of that is staggering."

"It's not losing the boy that we're worried about. The media will have a field day with that, I suspect. But I could tell just by watching the video that none of it was your fault."

"Thank God for small favors."

Leo shot him a hard look. "Trying to pass off a personal shopping trip as an official department program, on the other hand, that was stupid."

Ty nodded. He wanted to blame Doug Burke, but deep down he realized it had little to do with him. Ty had made the choice to misrepresent his shopping trip all on his own. For that, he supposed he deserved what he got. "How long?"

"Not sure. A few days. The media is going to be all over this. The chief wants to be ahead of it. The mayor agrees."

And here good old Evan had just looked him in the eye and shook his hand. The guy had always been smooth, even in high school. Apparently his step into politics had completed the package. "Next time I see Blankenship, remind me to thank him."

"Ty…"

He held up his hands. "I know. I know." Truth was, he understood Blankenship, Leo and the chief were just trying to protect the city and the department. But he felt a little hung out to dry. Even if he had caused it himself.

And he still couldn't shake the sense that this whole situation was not quite right.

MEGAN PULLED ON THE BLUE POLO shirt with Brilliance Cleaning emblazoned over the left breast and pulled her hair back into a ponytail. Her hands shook as she stretched the elastic hair band, and it took three tries for her to finally bind it tight enough so that wisps wouldn't escape in the first three seconds. She'd never been nervous about going to work before. Of course, she'd never planned to break all sorts of laws and betray her employer and his clients before, either.

She still couldn't believe any of this was real. Connor kidnapped. The ransom call. Her lying to police, to Ty. And soon she could add theft to the list. But as much as she didn't want to believe what she was about to do was real, it was. And as much as she didn't want to think about the possible ramifications of breaking the law this way, she knew she would be willing to do much worse if it meant getting her son back safe.

She pulled on her coat and gloves, grabbed her bag

and left the apartment, locking the door behind her. As she walked through the hall and down the steps, she couldn't help but remember taking this path with Connor every day on her way to drop him off with Mrs. Halverson in 1B while she cleaned. Last night, he'd been whining about wanting to wear shorts instead of his warm, fuzzy pajamas, and she'd been a little abrupt with him. When she got him home, safe and sound, she'd let him wear whatever he pleased. Never again would she waste time on petty arguments.

When she got him home...

She pushed out the door. Snow floated down in big flakes, clouds of it bright in the glow of the streetlights. An inch or maybe two had already fallen, coating the formerly clear sidewalks and streets and adding depth to the several inches that blanketed everywhere else.

She trudged to her car, cleared off the windows and drove out of the parking lot. The streets were slick, and for the first time, she had to force her mind off Connor and focus on driving. But as soon as she turned onto the quiet side street that led to Keating Security, she went back to wondering if her little boy had eaten dinner. Was he scared? Did he believe he would ever see her again?

The company's parking lot was dark and empty, just a few streetlights to highlight the falling snow. The security systems Keating Security placed in businesses around the area were electronically monitored, making it unnecessary for an employee to watch them full-time. The building was always empty when Megan showed up to clean.

She pushed her own door open and climbed out,

snugging the collar of her coat tight around her neck. There was nothing quieter than the world in the midst of a night snowstorm, and the intense hush gave her a chill that had little to do with the weather.

Was someone watching her?

She squinted into the night, but she could make out nothing but shadow and swirling white. Still, it could be possible the kidnapper was keeping tabs on her, making sure she followed through with his orders.

She hurried to the door. Still glancing around her, she stomped her feet free of snow, unlocked the glass door and slipped into the vestibule, closing and locking the door behind her. The alarm beeped its countdown. She punched the security code into the number pad to turn it off.

She wished she could engage the alarm while inside, but unfortunately that wasn't how this system was designed. Once the alarm was engaged, so were the interior motion sensors. One step and she'd set off an alarm herself. She'd just have to rely on the dead bolt on the door and get her business done quickly.

She opened the interior door and escaped into the halls, away from the glass exposing her to anyone who might be watching from the parking lot or street. Reaching the janitor's closet, she leaned on the door frame and let a breath shudder from her chest.

Her knees felt weak, and she had to concentrate to keep them from wobbling. The client files must be kept on secure servers that weren't linked to the internet, to prevent hacking. Otherwise, the kidnapper probably could have broken into the system remotely, and he'd have no need for her to use the access her job cleaning the building afforded her.

She hung the backpack vacuum on the handle of the garbage cart and pulled a cleaning kit off the shelf, as if she was going about her normal work routine. The chances of her being interrupted weren't good, but she wanted to be prepared just in case. As far as she knew, no one at Keating Security knew her background in computer systems. Why would they? As long as she was bonded, they had no reason to distrust her. Of course, Gary Burke knew. A second cousin of Doug's, he'd been charitable enough to give her a job with Brilliance Cleaning when her career had tanked in the middle of a tough economy. But he had contracts of his own to service. He rarely ever checked up on her. Either way, as long as she had the cleaning equipment handy, no one would think twice about finding her in one of the offices that housed the secure network.

It took her three offices to find a computer linked to the internal server. Situated in the corner of the building, the room felt uncomfortably exposed. Windows stretched along two walls, one peering out on the parking lot, the other on the adjacent wooded park. Again that feeling that someone was watching prickled over her skin. She moved to the side of one window and peered out.

Darkness stared back at her punctuated by white flakes swirling in the streetlights along the parking area's edge. She saw no vehicles, no movement. The forest side showed nothing but the skeletal shadows of trees barely visible through the snow.

The creepy feeling was probably caused by her guilty

conscience. She shivered and closed both sets of blinds anyway. She had to keep herself together. Find what she needed fast and get out.

Pulling a dusting wand from her kit for cover, she sat down at the desk, turned on the computer and focused on the monitor.

Password. She needed a password.

Her heart thumped so loud at first she thought it was heavy footsteps coming down the hall. She opened the desk drawer. Whether the company liked it or not, employees often kept their passwords written down and in easily accessed areas. With so many passwords for work programs and websites accessed at home, no one could keep all of them locked in their memories.

Sure enough, a small card was taped to the drawer's steel bottom, a collection of random letters and numbers printed on the card. She entered it onto the keyboard and a list of the company's clients popped up on the screen. She was in.

So far, so good.

She pulled out of her pocket a flash drive she'd brought from home and plugged it into a USB port. Now all she had to do was download the files for each client. She read over the names as she copied the list onto the drive.

A low rumble seemed to shake the building.

Her pulse jumped. She thrust up from the chair and stepped to the window. Splitting the blinds slightly with her fingers, she peered outside.

The yellow lights of a snowplow stuttered through the falling snow. It grumbled down the street and around a corner.

She let the blinds fall back into place, closed her eyes for a moment and focused on calming her racing pulse.

She made a horrible crook.

She sucked in a shaky breath and sat back down in front of the monitor. She had to focus on Connor, on getting him home safe, protecting her son. That's all she could let herself think about.

The client list was the easy part. She had no idea how long copying the actual specifications on each client's security system would take. She was only cleared to be in the building for a window of four hours, and if she hoped to cover her tracks, she needed to do at least a passable job of cleaning before her time ran out.

Another rumble came from outside.

Glancing out the corner of her eye in hopes that the sound was nothing but another snowplow, she clicked on the first client on the list, a pharmaceutical company. She directed the file to download to her flash drive.

The monitor went dark.

A surge of panic slammed through her. She clicked again, and the loud buzz of an alarm split the air.

Chapter Five

Ty had just stepped onto the snow-covered lawn of Keating Security when an alarm broke the white-blanketed stillness.

What the hell?

He slogged as fast as he could toward the building, wading through almost knee-deep snow. He'd followed Megan because he'd been worried about her. He'd left his sports car on the other side of a wooded park because he hadn't wanted her to know he was watching.

Could someone else have followed Megan, too? Had that person gotten into the building, seeking to harm her?

He broke through the deep powder and quickened his pace, racing across the parking lot, past Megan's car, up the walk to the front door. He yanked the handle.

It didn't budge.

He needed something heavy and hard. He ran back to Megan's car and tried the door. No luck. Remembering her old habit of locking her keys in the car, he slipped off his glove and skimmed his hand along the bottom edge of the front bumper. His fingers hit a small magnetic key box, and he pulled it free.

He slipped the key out and opened the ancient car's trunk. Peeling back the carpet, he focused on the spare tire…and the tire iron clamped beside it.

He pulled on his glove, grabbed the tire iron and returned to the entrance, testing the heft of the tool in his hand. He gave the glass a good rap at the level of the handle.

The alarm continued to blare, its hard buzz covering the sound of breaking glass. Cracks spiderwebbed across the window, the pieces at first sticking together. A few more raps, and he had punched out a hole.

He stuck a hand through. Feeling along the metal frame, he located the dead bolt lock, flicked it open and pushed through the door.

The alarm was louder inside the building. Its shriek blared through his head and lodged somewhere in the fillings of his back teeth. He took the hall leading to the office where he'd last spotted Megan through the trees, before she'd closed the blinds.

If an intruder had set off the alarm, he had no time to lose. Police would arrive eventually, but with the weather and resulting car wrecks and other emergencies, he couldn't be sure how soon they'd be able to make it.

He checked around the corner before stepping into the next hall. What he wouldn't give to have his gun, but he'd left his extra locked in the glove compartment of his car, and he didn't dare take the time to go back and get it. Armed with only a tire iron, he didn't relish running into whomever had set off the alarm. The tool was heavy enough to do some damage, but even so, it would be worthless against even a .22. He had to find Megan. He had to get her the hell out of here.

He burst into the office he'd noted from outside.

Megan was still there. But instead of cleaning, or trying to turn off an alarm or just about anything he expected, she was sitting in front of a computer screen, frantically tapping the keyboard. She jolted and stared at him with wide eyes. "Ty? What are you doing here?"

What was *he* doing? What was *she* doing? "Someone set off an alarm."

"I know."

"I was worried about you. When I left your apartment today something seemed...wrong."

She looked back down at the computer screen. Her fingers commenced their rapid-fire typing.

"Meg?"

"Not now. The police are going to be here any minute. I have to get what I can."

Had she lost her mind? "I am the police, Meg."

"You have to let me do this." She focused on him. "You have to help me."

"Do what? Help with what?" God knows, he'd help with whatever he could. "Tell me what is going on."

"I will. After. I'll explain it all."

Bits and pieces sifted into Ty's stunned mind. No one else was here? No one but Megan? "Who set off the alarm, Meg?"

Totally ignoring him, she leaned toward the monitor. "This can't happen. Damn, damn, damn."

"Did you set off the alarm?"

She made a low keening noise in her throat. Words, a crying sound, he couldn't tell among the din. After a second, she rocked back a little in her chair, her eyes still on the blank screen. "Honestly?"

"Please."

"Yes. I set off the alarm. I missed an extra layer of security. I can't believe I missed it. I can't believe..." She leaned closer and started tapping again, as if she was willing the computer to do whatever it was she wanted.

"What are you doing?"

"I'll explain later."

He flattened his palm over her moving fingers. "You'll explain now."

She looked up at him for the first time since he'd burst into the office. Desperation gleamed in her eyes. Tears streamed silently down her cheeks. "I'm trying to steal confidential client files. Specs on their security systems. But I haven't gotten much. The security on each separate file...I didn't expect that."

"You're...why?"

"I don't know," she yelled over the alarm's buzz. "I wasn't thinking, I guess. I was so panicked about getting the files, I didn't think it through."

Obviously he needed to be more clear. "Why are you stealing files?" Just asking the question felt ridiculous, but he sensed there was a serious explanation behind it. There had to be.

"I got a call."

"From whom?" he asked.

"I didn't recognize the voice. But he said he had

Connor. He said if I stole these files, if I gave them to him, I could get Connor back."

Now he was really confused. With the alarm blaring in his ears, maybe he hadn't heard her quite right. "I thought Doug had Connor."

"No. We lied about that."

He'd known she was lying, but he'd never guessed the lie was about Connor being safe. "Why?"

"I'll explain it all. Really, I will. And then you can arrest me or whatever you're going to do. But right now, the whole system has shut itself down, and if I can't get it back up, I won't be able to copy anything."

He didn't know any of the details, but he knew Megan, and what she was saying made a strange kind of sense. Her little boy's safety was the only thing that could ever make her go to such extremes. To protect her son, she'd do anything.

The question he had to answer was, what was *he* going to do?

A jitter lodged in his chest. He was a cop, through and through. It was all he ever wanted to be. All he probably could be, and yet...

The alarm stopped.

Ty slumped with relief. Even though his ears still rang with ghosts of sound, at least he could now hear himself think. "You got back in?"

"No. I just shut off the alarm. The rest isn't working. It's not working."

The defeated tone in her voice gave him a hollow feeling at the base of his throat. "You're sure?"

Her fingers stilled. "I screwed up. I screwed up. I

tripped the security, and now the client database has totally shut down. I've never worked with a system like this before. I don't know what to do."

Red and blue lights flashed through the closed blinds on the parking lot side, first from a distance, then closer until the whole room pulsed with color.

"They'll know it was me. I had to use my number to get into the building."

"No one will have to look that far. Your car is parked out front. They're probably already running your plates."

She focused on him, eyes wide as if the fix she was in had just become real. "What do I do?"

He needed time. Time to think. A luxury he didn't have. The officer outside was likely assessing the broken door this very moment, waiting for backup to arrive before he came inside.

Time—for fiddling with the computer, for weighing decisions, for regretting the action he was about to take— was over. If he was honest with himself, there was only one decision he could make. He'd lost Connor. He had to do whatever it took to get the little boy back. And he had to do his best to protect Megan in the process. "The police will be inside any minute. Unless you want guns drawn on you, we need to get out there, explain things."

"Explain things? How?"

A good damn question. "Just follow my lead." He tried to interject confidence into his voice, but it sounded flat even to his own ears. He just hoped he could come up with something in the next few seconds.

JUST FOLLOW HIS LEAD. JUST follow his lead.

Megan repeated the words in her head, but she didn't feel any more confident than when Ty had said them the first time. So she'd face the police, explain what she was doing, and then what? Even though she hadn't been successful in stealing anything, she would take the blame for it all the same. And then what would happen to Connor?

"Ready?" Ty said, gesturing out the office door.

"Wait."

She ducked back to the computer, pulled out her flash drive and jammed it in her pocket. All that was on it was a client list, but at least it was something. It proved she'd tried. Although she had serious doubts that someone willing to kidnap a little boy would award her extra points for effort.

On the way out to the hall, Ty paused. He pointed to the cleaning equipment she'd hauled into the office for cover in case she was found. "Is that a vacuum cleaner?"

"Yes." She had to admit, the device looked more like a jet pack from some old sci-fi movie than a piece of cleaning equipment. "You wear it like a backpack."

He grabbed the device, slung it over one shoulder, the hose dangling down his back, and strode into the hall.

She followed him out through the entry vestibule. Broken glass crunching under the soles of her shoes, she eyed the damage Ty wreaked in order to get into the building and cringed.

They met two officers the moment they stepped outside the company's front entrance. One had gray sparkling through his dark hair and mustache. The other was clean shaven and had a case of acne that would make a teenager cringe.

Megan held her breath and prayed they wouldn't ask her anything. She had no idea what she would say if they did. She just had to trust Ty would lead and she'd know how to follow when the time came.

The older one eyed Ty and arched his eyebrows in surprise. "Davis? You working night shift without telling me?"

Ty chuckled, the laugh sounding so relaxed and real, Megan glanced at him. Ty gestured to the backpack vac. "Helping out a friend. Ed, Trevor, this is Megan Garvey."

They exchanged pleased-to-meet-yous. Megan forced herself to meet the men's eyes as she shook their hands.

"Helping a friend? How are you helping?" Ed frowned at the vacuum as if he wasn't sure what the thing was.

"Megan works for Brilliance Cleaning. She's had a rough day, so I volunteered to do a little vacuuming. But as it turns out, I'm not doing much helping tonight."

"You're the one who set off the alarm?"

"Afraid so." Ty nodded to the broken window and held up the aluminum vacuum wand. "Turns out that entry area is more cramped, this thing is more lethal and I'm much more clumsy than I ever imagined."

The younger cop chuckled. But the older one didn't seem to find it quite so funny. "It takes a lot of force to break through glass like that."

Megan's legs vibrated, as if at any moment, they could

just give out and send her crashing to the concrete. She didn't know how much Ty knew about security systems. Heck, she hadn't thought too much about the systems at Keating herself. She'd been more concerned with cleaning water spots from the faucets and making sure the trash can liners fit. But after tonight, it was obvious that the company had installed different alarm systems on their doors and on their computers. The question was whether or not they would show up as two different types of breaches when the system automatically contacted police.

"It wasn't Ty. He was just trying to cover for me. I set off the alarm." She could feel Ty watching her, and she hoped he figured out what she was doing. "I used one of the computers to try to go online."

"Really?" The older cop's eyes seemed to burn straight through her. "Why would you do that?"

The lie turned to dust in her throat. She searched her mind, but nothing was there.

"You guys hear about the child abduction this morning at Lakewood Mall?" Ty asked. "Megan's son was the boy kidnapped today."

"Garvey." The older cop's focus swung from Ty back to Megan. "I'm sorry. Your name should have rung a bell. Guess I'm getting old."

"I'll say," the younger cop said under his breath.

"They found the boy. He's with his father. But it's been kind of a rough day, as you can imagine. And when the alarm went off, I overreacted a bit."

Officer Ed stroked his mustache with thumb and forefinger. "And broke the door with that vacuum tube?"

"Or maybe a tire iron." Ty shrugged. "I was worried."

The younger cop laughed out loud. "You've always been the jumpy sort, Davis."

Ty chuckled, the sound of relief palpable. "You'll record this as a false alarm then? A simple mistake? I'll pay to replace the door, of course."

"That would probably help the situation," Officer Ed agreed.

"Sorry we had to drag you out here for no reason."

Ed waved away the apology. "Better than having a reason. I'm sure the owner will feel the same way."

Megan wasn't sure of that. Not sure at all. But as long as the officers had bought their story, she couldn't complain. Now that she had another chance, she just hoped she could find a way to override the security shutdown and get to those files. "Thank you, officer. So can we finish cleaning now?"

Ed shook his mostly silver head. "Afraid not. At least not until an owner or manager arrives. He'll have to sign off before we can let you back in the building."

Megan felt sick. "He's coming out here tonight?"

He glanced at his watch. "Unless he had a problem with the roads, he should be here any minute."

ANTHONY KEATING WASN'T HAPPY to be dragged out into the snowstorm at ten at night, and he made his displeasure clear to everyone involved. But it wasn't until Megan's own boss from the cleaning company showed up that she finally let go of all hope of getting her hands on those files.

Gary Burke might have been Doug's second cousin, but he looked nothing like her ex-husband. Big and doughy around the middle, he wore his hair military short and his beard mountain man long. He blustered into what little lobby Keating Security had and marched straight past Megan without giving her a glance. He disappeared into Keating's office.

Megan glanced at Ty. The police officers had left when Keating arrived, but Ty had stayed even after he'd made his case to Keating and promised to pay for the door. "You don't have to stay."

"I know."

Minute stretched after minute. Finally Anthony Keating walked past them and out of the building, and Gary poked his head into the hall. "Megan? Can I have a word with you?"

Heat infused her cheeks. She had a bad feeling she knew what was coming. She could only hope some of the sympathy the officers had shown had rubbed off.

She followed him into Keating's spacious office. Even though the room was well-appointed, with soft leather chairs and a small couch, she hovered just inside the door, preferring to face her boss on her feet. "You talked to the police?"

"I talked to Keating," he boomed. "What happened tonight? He said you tried to use a computer? Why would you do something like that?"

"My son..." She hated using Connor as an excuse, but at least the story was accurate...in a way. "He went missing today. At least we thought he did for a little while, but it ended up that he was with Doug. I just wanted to send him an email before he went to bed."

Bushy brows pulled low over Gary's eyes. "Keating says the computer you used did not have an internet connection."

She swallowed. Her throat felt parched and she realized for the first time that she hadn't had anything to eat or drink all day. "It was a mistake. I didn't realize…I shouldn't have used a client's computer. It won't happen again."

"You used the wrong computer? You expect me to believe you didn't know the difference?"

"I was still upset. I wasn't thinking." She tried to sound innocent, honest, but she'd forgotten exactly what that felt like. Her voice sounded more nervous than anything, chattering too high, too fast.

Gary shook his head. "I realize the police don't know much about you, Megan, but I do."

A hum rose in her ears. Her heart leaped into double time.

"You can tell those officers you accidently used the wrong computer to get on the internet, but you can't feed that excuse to me." His voice lowered, sounding more tired than angry.

She pulled in a breath and held it. She had to somehow talk her way out of this. She had to get another crack at that computer system. But for the life of her, she couldn't think of a way to justify hacking into a client's secure computer system. At least not a justification Gary would buy.

The truth.

She couldn't dare lay out the facts for her boss, could she? She'd just succeeded in getting law enforcement away from this case. If Gary knew she was dealing with a kidnapper, he wouldn't let her access those computers, he'd call the police. And if he did that, everything would be over.

"I screwed up. I'm sorry. It won't happen again."

Gary let out a heavy sigh and crossed his arms over his belly. "I'm sorry too, Megan. I really am. But Tony Keating doesn't want you cleaning this place anymore, and I have to say, I can't blame him."

She'd known the words were coming, but they hit her like a fist anyway. Now what was she going to do? "I understand. I'll finish up tonight and turn in my keys."

"I'll need your keys now." He held out a big hand. "Tony has already changed the security code, so I'll finish up the cleaning tonight."

She figured he wouldn't let her have one last night, but she had to try all the same. "I have some personal things in the janitor's closet." She wasn't sure how a trip to the janitor's closet would buy her enough time to try the computers again, but it was all she could come up with.

"I'll collect them for you. And Megan?"

She choked back her despair and willed her voice to function. "Yes?"

"I'm so sorry. Really, I am. I hate to do this, but…" He paused and dropped his gaze to the office floor, as if he couldn't quite go on.

Megan didn't know what he was building up to, but she was hard pressed to care. Without access to that computer system, there was no way she could come up with the files the kidnapper demanded. Without the files, she'd never see her son again. Gary didn't know it, but he'd already taken from her everything that mattered. He couldn't hurt her anymore than he already had. "What is it, Gary? Go ahead."

"I can't have an employee of mine breaking into a client's computer. I'm afraid I'm going to have to let you go."

She was wrong. He *could* hurt her more. He could take away her livelihood. But compared to the risk to her son, losing her job was way down on her list.

"You okay?"

"I'll be fine, Gary. Just fine."

He nodded. "You could have gone to jail for what you did. You know that, don't you? You're getting out of this easy."

Easy? Not exactly. She'd go to jail willingly if only she knew Connor would be safe. "Good night, Gary."

She forced her feet to carry her past him and out of the office, down the hall and away from her only chance to save her son. The lobby was empty, and although she'd told Ty to leave before she'd been called in to talk to Gary, she found herself wishing he was still there.

She passed the temporarily patched window and pushed out into the storm. The wind had kicked up since she and Ty had last stepped outside to talk to the officers, and flakes pelted her cheeks, stinging like cold needles. Tears flooded her eyes. One moment of distraction, one mistake, and she'd made everything so much worse. And now…now she had run out of options.

Once again, she was on her own with nowhere to turn.

She raised her face to the storm. There by her car stood Ty, coat pulled up around his ears, snowflakes glistening in his dark hair. "Don't look so shocked. I said I would help you get Connor back. I meant it."

She wiped the tears from her cheeks with the back of one glove. She knew she should say something, but she had no idea what.

"I only have one condition. That you tell me the truth from here on out. You've got to trust me. Deal?"

She bobbed her head in a nod and willed her voice to work. "Deal."

Chapter Six

Ty let up on the accelerator and eased around the bend in the road as Megan's car hugged the turn. The ancient little junker was surprisingly good in the snow. Better than his car. But even so, the roads were getting brutal, one moment slick as ice, the next snow deep as quicksand. With all that she'd gone through today, he was glad he had offered to drive.

He'd pick up his car in the morning.

This whole situation was crazy. Connor kidnapped. Megan trying to steal sensitive security information. He hadn't asked her what had happened with her boss. He hadn't needed to. As soon as he saw the expression on her face, he knew things had gone badly. Not that he imagined for a second that everything would turn out okay. Once that alarm went off, he had three choices. Turn Megan in, run or face the consequences. And since neither one of them was cut out for the first two options, he'd figured things might get ugly.

The question now was what to do next. He had the answer. Convincing Megan to agree was the tricky part.

He took the upcoming turn onto Forest Avenue. The

street was fully decked out for the holidays. Twinkle lights festooned every light pole and danced over nearly every roofline and porch all the way down the block. They drove past Harris House—Dee Dee Harris the heiress's home—each window of the sprawling stone Victorian featuring a wreath robed in new snow. The cast iron fence flanking the huge property was roped with heavy swags of evergreen and white lights. Snowflakes swirled in the air, making the scene feel magical.

Ty doubted Megan saw any of it. She stared out the window, but there was a blankness to her eyes, a faraway expression on her face. She wrapped her arms around her middle as if she was chilled, even though the car's heater was roaring full blast.

No doubt, she was thinking of Connor.

"We'll find a way to get him back, Meg." He could feel her turn to face him, and he wished he could hold her gaze. But with the roads getting worse by the second, even here in town, he only dared steal short glances. "We will."

"I was fired tonight."

That was what he'd been afraid of. "I'm sorry."

"I'm not worried about the job. I'll find another job. But Keating...I can't get back in the building."

Ty nodded. His plan didn't involve returning to the building, but he couldn't spring it on her out of the blue. He'd be asking a lot of her. She would have to trust others, let them handle things. She wouldn't like it. He knew that. He had to make his argument carefully if he wanted to convince her it was the best way. "What if we could get Connor back without the Keating Security files?"

"How?"

He knew her willingness to listen hinged on how he worded this next bit. And before he made his pitch, he wanted to be sure he understood the situation. Easier to do when not trying to yell over an ear-splitting alarm. "First you need to explain some things. Start from the beginning. The kidnapper. He called you?"

She nodded.

"When?"

"Back at my apartment when I told you Doug called me? It was really him."

He knew she'd been hiding something. But hearing for certain that she'd lied straight to his face and about so much...he gripped the wheel harder. "What did he say?"

"To get the police out of my apartment. He said if I didn't, I wouldn't see Connor again."

"Did he tell you how to do that?"

"He suggested I convince you everything was okay. That Doug had Connor. Or someone else who was trustworthy."

Trustworthy. Not a word he'd use to describe Doug Burke. But then, he wasn't exactly unbiased...and he knew Doug's history. "And Doug, he went along with the lie?"

"He didn't want to at first. He was afraid he might get in trouble with police."

"But you convinced him?"

"He's worried about Connor, too."

"So what happens when someone from the department checks in on Doug and learns he doesn't have Connor? Because they can't just drop this without confirming that your son is okay."

She paused. Only the rhythm of windshield wipers and whir of the heater fan filled the car. "We were thinking that wouldn't be necessary. Or if it was, I could get Connor back before then. I promised Doug I'd get him back."

Obviously that part of the equation had changed, and now Megan was beating herself up for it. "Leo told me Doug was out of town."

She nodded. "He's saying they're at a hotel in Milwaukee, that he's planning to take Connor to the children's museum there. We thought it was better than saying he took Connor to Chicago with him. We weren't sure what would happen if he admitted to crossing state lines."

So if Doug didn't come back to Lake Hubbard, Leo would have to send someone to Milwaukee to check Doug's story. "This storm will certainly delay the police's follow-up."

"How long?"

"Hard to say. Once the snow stops, the road crews work pretty quickly. As soon as someone can get over there, they will."

She stared out the windshield again, and for a second, he let himself take a glance at her profile. Her high cheekbones. Her tiny nose that turned up ever so slightly at the tip. And those kind eyes, long lashes and waves of auburn hair. Megan was beautiful, sure, but she was much more than that. More than a man could ever want in any woman. And not for the first time in the many years he'd known Megan Garvey, he wished they would have first met when they were just a little older. When he was ready for a real relationship and not just a spin at a teenage crush.

"I wish we didn't have to do all this guessing. We'd be so much further ahead if I could just come out and ask Leo what's going on." He again glanced her way, looking for a reaction.

She was watching him, a crease digging between her eyebrows. "What are you suggesting?"

"You need to let the department handle it."

Out of the corner of his eye, he could see her shaking her head. "He'll hurt Connor. That's what he said. If I don't do everything as he wants, I won't see my son again."

"Everything he wants is the security information for Keating's clients?"

"Right. And the police *not involved*."

"You don't have the information, do you?"

Her gaze dropped to her lap. "No."

"Then giving him everything he wants is no longer a possibility. Getting the police involved is our best choice."

"It's not *our* choice to make. It's *my* choice."

"You're right. You're right. It's your choice." He had to remember he was merely helping. He couldn't take this problem off Megan's hands, as much as he wished he could. He'd lost her son, but Meg was the only one who could get him back. He just wanted more than anything to find Connor. And the best way he knew to help was to bring all the resources of law enforcement to bear.

He focused on the road. The snow was coming down so heavy now, it was hard to see a half block in front of the bumper. But navigating the snowstorm was simple next to what Megan was going through.

She wrapped her arms tighter around herself. "What would they do?"

"We can bring in experts in abductions. We can request help from the FBI."

"But they aren't going to let me deliver the real security information. What would they do, have me deliver a blank flash drive?"

"I don't know. But you'd have resources behind you. People who have dealt with this kind of thing before."

"I just keep hearing what he said. I'm just afraid…."

"I think getting law enforcement on our side gives us the best chance." If he was honest, he'd say the only chance, but he sensed Megan couldn't deal with that right now.

She dropped her gaze to her lap and let out a heavy breath.

One block, a right turn and two more blocks and they'd be at the police station, the place he'd been heading from the first, as long as he could talk Megan into reason before they got there. "We can go to the station right now. You can get help with this. The kidnapper will never know. What do you say?"

The bleat of her cell phone cut through the tension in the car. She looked up at him, eyes glowingly green in the dashboard lights. "It's him."

MEGAN'S HEARTBEAT STUTTERED. She zipped open her bag and dug inside. Her fingers shook as they closed around her cell phone. She pulled it out, jabbed the answer button with a finger, and brought the phone to her ear. "Hello?"

"I hear there was a mishap at Keating Security tonight. The police were called. You wouldn't know anything about that, would you?"

That voice. The same one. She'd known it was him, but the gruff tone still gave her a jolt. "It was a mistake."

"And you expect me to believe that?"

"It's the truth."

"The truth? I told you, no police."

"I didn't mean for that to happen. You've got to believe me."

"I don't *got* to do anything. But you do…if you want to keep your son alive. And the first thing I told you to do was stay away from the police."

A tremor seized her. She sucked in a deep breath, then let it out slowly. She had to stay calm. He couldn't know Ty had been talking about going to the police just a moment ago. He couldn't have seen them driving together. She had to think. "I am staying away from police. I didn't tell them anything."

"Why should I believe you?" the voice rasped in her ear. "You could be with the cops right now."

She focused on Ty. Her chest tightened until she had to struggle for each breath. Could the kidnapper see her? Did he know she was with Ty? Or was he just reacting to the police being called to Keating Security? How much did he know?

Ty swung the car to the curb and stopped. He twisted in his seat and met her gaze.

She held on to it. He was a cop. She couldn't risk being near him. And yet as much as she hated relying on other people, she didn't know how she'd handle this alone. She'd done a pretty poor job so far. "I'm in my car."

Ty's lips formed an unspoken word.

At first she didn't recognize what he was trying to tell her. But the second time his mouth formed the shapes, she caught on. Connor. Ask about Connor.

She nodded and he brought his head close to hers. Angling the phone slightly away from her ear so Ty could hear, she pushed the demand from her lips. "I need to know Connor is okay. I want to speak to him."

"Now why would I let you do that? You haven't done one thing I've told you. Not one thing. You get me those files, then you can talk to the boy."

"I can't—"

Ty's eyes widened, and he shook his head.

Her throat tightened. "I can't do anything until I know Connor is okay. I want to talk to him."

Ty nodded.

She waited for the answer. Her pulse beat loud in her ears. The phone felt slick in her hand.

"Mommy?" The voice was strong and soft and unbearably sweet.

She pressed the phone tight to her ear. "Connor. Baby. Everything's okay, sweetie." Her voice trembled and broke, disintegrating into a choked sob.

"Mommy!" Connor's voice rose.

He hadn't sounded frightened at first, but now he did. The sound of it scraped up her spine and drove into her chest. "It's okay, baby. I'll make things okay."

"Yes, you will." The voice was back, and with it a chill wrapped around Megan, a cold she could never shake. "But the only way you can make things okay is if you do everything I say. And I mean everything."

She willed her voice to function, to sound strong. "I've run into a glitch in the security system. It's going to take longer."

"I don't have the time to mess with excuses. If you can't deliver, I'll have to cut my losses and find someone else who can."

What did that mean, *cut his losses?* "No, please. I'll get it to you. But it might take a little time. The system is—"

"The system is your problem. How do I know you aren't stalling for time while you have the police looking for me?"

"I'm not. I swear." Her chest ached, her heart pumping so hard, she thought it might explode. Hadn't she been ready to do just that?

Tears blurred her vision, transforming the car's interior into a watery mash of shadow. She blinked, trying to see clearly. "I'll get the information to you as soon as I can. I promise."

Ty brought his hand to her chin and gently turned her face toward him. He mouthed something else. *Where?*

"Where do you want me to send it?"

"I'll call tomorrow night to let you know."

One day. She only had twenty-four hours.

"And just in case you're planning to turn this number over to the police, this phone is not traceable, so don't waste your time. You don't have much of it left."

The signal went dead.

For a moment, Megan sat still, holding the phone to her ear, trying to compose herself, to let what had just happened sink in. Her baby. She'd heard her baby's voice. Her chest, her arms, every cell in her body ached to hold his little body.

"How much time did he give you?"

"He's going to call tomorrow night."

"Then we'd better get going." He shifted the car into Drive and pulled out into the snow-covered street. He took the next right, still heading in the direction of the police station.

"Stop."

He glanced at Megan, his brows arching in silent question.

"I said, stop. I'm not going to the police station."

"Megan, we talked about this. You have to let us help. It's the best way."

"I can't take the risk. I won't."

"You mean you won't take help. Don't do this, Megan. You can't handle this alone."

"Maybe you're right. Maybe I can't. But I'm going to have to try."

"You don't have to do this his way."

"Every time I come near a police officer, he seems to know."

"He can't—"

"He does."

"The thing at Keating Security. That was called out by a dispatcher. Anyone with a police band radio could have picked that up. And he could have been watching your apartment after he took Connor. Neither one of those things means he has some kind of super surveillance power."

"And the fact that you were just heading toward the police station when he called?"

"He didn't mention anything about the police station, did he? Don't you think he would have if he'd known? Don't you think he'd mention me, if he somehow was watching us?"

She tried to calm her breathing. Ty had a point. She was probably letting her fear and imagination get the best of her. But when it came down to choosing to risk her son that way, no amount of logical explanation mattered. "You didn't hear Connor. You don't know. I'm not going to the police station."

He blew a breath through tight lips.

The police station loomed ahead, a beige concrete box of a building built in the sixties. A single squad car sat in the small parking lot in front, the others probably out patrolling the street or in a garage where they wouldn't have to be shoveled out of the snow. Ty drove steady, neither too fast for the conditions nor too slow.

He continued past the station.

They drove two more blocks in silence before Ty spoke. "You might not be willing to go to the police, Megan. That's your choice. I understand it. But if you think you're going to do this all on your own, you're wrong. Connor was kidnapped under my nose, and I'm going to see that he gets back to you safe. And about that, you have no choice."

Chapter Seven

Ty hadn't had a woman over to his house for a month or more, and the bachelor pigsty showed it. He picked the dirty uniform off the couch and swept his hand over the cushions to clear them of corn chip crumbs or stray popcorn. He took Megan's damp coat and his as well, and hung them on the backs of his two kitchen chairs to dry. He wasn't very diligent about cleaning his bathroom even on a good day, so he didn't want to think about that. Instead, he washed two water glasses and sloshed some whiskey into them. He carried them to the living room and offered one to Megan.

She held up a hand, palm out. "No, thanks."

"It's not much. It will take the edge off. Go ahead. You need it." He didn't have great hopes of either of them sleeping tonight, but a shot of whiskey might at least help them relax a little.

She took the glass and cradled it in both hands but resisted bringing it to her lips.

He sat on the couch beside Megan and sipped his booze, savoring its slow burn. It had been a long and horrible day, and it wasn't over yet. Before either of them pretended to sleep, they had to work out what they were going to do next.

Megan set her untouched drink on the side table. "I appreciate your help, Ty. Really, I do. But this isn't going to work."

He didn't ask why, merely raised his brows.

"He said no police," Megan answered. "I doubt someone who would kidnap a child would make an exception."

"He doesn't have to know I'm involved. Besides, I'm not a cop right now."

"What do you mean?"

He hadn't been going to tell her about his conversation with Leo. He hadn't wanted to worry her. But if it would convince her to let him help, it was worth spilling. "I've been suspended pending an investigation."

"An investigation? Of you? Oh my God, Ty."

He shook his head. Leave it to Megan to be concerned about him, even in the midst of what she faced. The woman was slow to accept anything from anyone, especially him, but she wasn't afraid to give. "I don't want you to think about it. It's just procedure. A way to keep the media satisfied and off the department and the city's back."

"That doesn't seem very fair."

Of course the actual abduction wasn't what the department was concerned about. Not that he planned to explain to Megan what the suspension was actually for. "They just don't want to give the media anything to feed on."

"The media can't blame you, either."

He shrugged a shoulder. TV news, radio talk shows, even the newspaper, they were interested in whatever made a story. And this? Christmas, fear of strangers and a police officer at fault…it was like Santa himself had plopped a big juicy story smack in the media's stocking. "Don't worry about me. Seriously. As long as we can get Connor back, I don't really care about the rest. And neither should you."

She nodded, but she didn't look totally convinced. "So you're okay with me not going to police? Trying to steal those security files tonight? You won't report any of it?"

"I'm never going to be okay with it. But won't report it, no."

"Even if I have to do other things before this is over?"

What could he say? "Even then."

She let out a long breath and picked up her whiskey glass from the table, her relief palpable.

Too bad he didn't feel the same way. How could he when he was pretty sure it was the worst decision he'd ever made? No, he'd made another bad one five years ago, and this time he wasn't going to abandon Megan when she needed him. Even if she pushed him away. "Maybe we can make sure *other things* aren't necessary."

"How?"

"Did you get anything before the system shut down?"

"Just a list of Keating's clients. I don't see how that's going to tell us anything."

"It might be able to tell us quite a bit. If we're lucky."

She pressed her lips into a flat line and stared at the still untasted whiskey in her hand.

He took another slug from his own glass, trying to organize his thoughts, figure out if he actually had a strategy or was just grasping at straws. "We come at this from a different angle. If we can find out why the kidnapper wants this information, what business or businesses he's targeting, then maybe we can figure out who he is."

"Keating has a number of clients. Seems like kind of a long shot."

"Maybe, maybe not. Let's see the list." He strode into his extra bedroom and grabbed his laptop. Once back in the living room, he fired it up and handed it to Megan. She pulled the flash drive from her pocket and plugged it in.

She brought up the list on the screen and tilted the computer toward him.

He ran his gaze down the list of businesses. With some, it was obvious what business they were in. Ellenston Pharmaceuticals. Radiant Diamonds. Morgan's Artisan Cheese. Others weren't quite so obvious. "What is H&V?"

"A clothing wholesaler."

"How do you know that?"

"They have a warehouse near my house in Chicago. Once a year they'd hold sample sales. Nothing fancy. Just sweatshirts, T-shirts, that kind of thing."

"Okay." He picked out another name on the list. "Julianne's?"

"I have no idea."

He dashed back into the spare room and grabbed a notebook. Returning to the couch, he scribbled down the name. "How about IGB Data? Data mining? A credit reporting agency?"

"I don't know."

Another note. "Fortune Gaming?"

"That's from across the border, too. They run some of the offtrack betting in the Chicago area."

Interesting. "The mob could be involved in something like that."

Megan's eyes grew wide. "You think this might have something to do with the mafia?"

"I hope not. But they've been known to do things like kidnapping." He hated to bring up the possibility, but it was probably best Megan faced things straight out. Maybe if there was mob involvement in this, she would agree to talk to the FBI.

He moved his gaze farther down the list, jotting down a few more names that needed checking out. He paused on a name that was far too familiar.

"What is it?" Megan leaned close enough that he could smell the light scent of her shampoo.

"Keating provides security for Harris House."

"Evan and Dee Dee? You're sure?"

He scanned the rest of the list. "It seems to be one of only a handful of residences, all in that same neighborhood. Of course it's probably the biggest and most opulent residence in the county."

"True. And Keating is probably the biggest security company in the county, too. But I wonder..." She glanced up at him, her face only inches from his, and for a moment, the idea of kissing her flashed through his mind.

Probably not the best timed thought he'd ever had. "Wonder what?"

"Something Evan Blankenship told me this afternoon. He said if I needed help getting Connor back, I should come to him."

After the way she'd resisted his help the past several hours, the thought of her running to Blankenship made Ty a little queasy. Okay, a lot queasy. When it came right down to it, it was too reminiscent of what had happened years ago. "Megan? What are you thinking?"

She shot him a look. "Maybe he could get me back into Keating."

"So you can steal security files, including the information for the system in Evan Blankenship's own home, and give them to a criminal?"

"I didn't think about it that way."

Megan was desperate, and she had good reason to feel that way. Guilt niggled at the back of his mind. If he was honest with himself, he had to admit his main objection had little to do with the law and a lot to do with uncomfortable echoes from the past.

He pressed his lips into a somber smile he hoped she would accept as something of an apology. "We'll figure something out."

He nodded at the laptop's screen, eager to get her mind working on something else. "Out of the names on this list, what raises red flags for you?"

"Red flags?"

"Which places do you see as a target for a break-in?"

She skewed her lips to the side as if chewing on the inside of her cheek. "The pharmaceutical company might be a target. I've heard prescription drugs are pretty popular as street drugs, anyway."

He nodded. "That's a good one."

"And the jewelry store, of course. And if the data company actually compiles credit information, that might be a good bet."

Megan may not be in law enforcement, but she was sharp. Those were exactly the ones he'd picked out at first glance. "So we know we're probably not looking for someone who's interested in stealing artisan cheeses."

Megan gave him a weak smile.

It was a groan-worthy joke, he knew. He was trying to lighten things up, but he should have saved his breath. "We'll get him back, Meg."

She looked away from him. Her eyes glistened in the lamplight.

He'd never seen her look this way before, so utterly... defeated. Megan had always been so strong. So independent. She'd gone through hell with her parents, and still she'd soldiered on. She'd never seemed to need anybody, especially not him. Even though when he looked back on those times, he knew she had...and that he'd let her down.

The past was the past, yet to see her like this now made him want to be there for her more than ever. He set the laptop on the coffee table, slid closer to her and slipped an arm around her shoulders.

She placed a palm on his chest. "I…I can't."

"I just want to hold you. That's all." That wasn't all, of course. He wanted to kiss her, make love to her. He'd been wanting all of those things since seeing her again this morning. Maybe since he'd returned from the police academy five years ago and found her engaged to Doug Burke. But even he knew enough not to push that far. "I want to do something to make you feel better…less alone."

She shook her head. "There's nothing that you can do."

No, of course there wasn't. Nothing short of bringing her son home. "I'll stick with you this time, Megan. Through this whole thing. We'll get him back."

MEGAN SOAKED IN THE FEEL OF him through her fingertips. The woven texture of his shirt. The solidness of the chest beneath.

She'd been so focused on Connor, on getting her son back, that she hadn't really considered how much she was asking of Ty. Since Connor had been taken, he had been there for her, just like he was promising again now. Each time she'd needed him to cover up for her, he'd done it. Even if it had meant lying to the police, risking his career, even breaking the law. He'd stuck by her, regardless of how much it could cost him.

And somehow that made her feel more unbalanced than anything else.

She pulled her hand away and tangled her fingers together in her lap. "I know your career is at stake. You've done so much to help me, things that could get you in serious trouble. I know you feel responsible, but—"

"I *am* responsible." He blew a breath through tense lips. Reaching out, he enfolded her hand in both of his. "I lost Connor. You've been very generous about not blaming me for it, but it's the truth. But even if I hadn't, I would help you, Megan. So if you're going to try to talk me out of it, don't. I'm doing it for myself as much as I'm doing it for you."

She dropped her gaze to her lap, to her hand embraced by his. She had to admit, she was glad he was with her. She didn't know how long or what it meant, but it felt good to not be facing this alone. "I'm sorry, Ty. I'm just not very good at this."

He let out a laugh. "Good at this? You think anyone is good at having their child kidnapped?"

"Of course not. I meant I'm not good at accepting help. Over the past few years, I've gotten used to doing things on my own."

"It's not just the past few years."

She brought her gaze back to his face. "What?"

"You never were very good at accepting help, actually. At least not from me."

She frowned.

"What? You don't remember that Christmas before I left for the police academy? Insisting on cleaning out your parents' house all on your own?"

Of course, she did. She'd spent most of that horrible December packing up hers and her mother's clothing and getting rid of everything she could in order to trim down their collection of household belongings to apartment size. Her dad had promised he'd help, but he'd never shown up. No surprise there. And Mom, of course, she hadn't been able. So the move had been up to Megan alone. "That seems so long ago." And yet very little had changed. She was still reticent about accepting help from Ty. She didn't know how long he'd be around. She was always more comfortable going it alone.

Ty nodded. "It was a long time ago."

"I wasn't trying to be difficult, though. It was just my way to work through some things." Her way to have control over something that holiday. Anything.

"I know it was tough on you, I just wish…I don't know, that I could have been there for you, I guess."

"You had your own stuff to pack." He'd been getting ready to leave for the police academy. He'd been excited about the future before him. She had been trying to clean up the messy pain of her past. "We were in two different worlds."

"My timing was terrible. I still feel bad about that."

She took a deep breath. She didn't like to dwell on those days. She didn't want to think of them now.

"With your mom in the hospital and everything else, I should have waited. A year, two, whatever it took. I shouldn't have left you to Doug Burke."

"No. Don't say that."

"Why not?"

"First of all, Doug and I had Connor. And I wouldn't change that for the world."

"Okay. Fair enough. And second?"

"You're a cop, Ty. You had to go to the academy,

especially when you got your way paid. It's what you were always meant to do."

"Delaying the academy for a year wouldn't have prevented me from becoming a cop."

"It also wouldn't have changed anything between us." It was a hard truth, and not one she wanted to admit to herself, let alone Ty. She knew saying it would hurt him. But his romanticized view of those days wasn't realistic. And trying to rewrite the past wouldn't get either of them anywhere.

"How do you know it wouldn't have changed things? How can you say that?"

"Because you were only twenty. You weren't ready to settle down. Not back then."

His lips pressed into a line.

That wasn't all of it, of course. But the rest…she shook her head. The past was done. She didn't want to dwell on it. Not when it took all the energy she had to be ready for what the future might throw at her. "I knew what I was getting into when I married Doug. I didn't just fall into his arms because you were gone."

He looked up to the ceiling and took a deep breath. When he returned his gaze to hers, his face held a resigned calm that made her want to cry. "You're probably right," he said. "I wasn't ready to settle down. But you deserved more than Doug Burke. I still wish I'd have gotten the chance to prove that to you."

The room grew watery. She blinked back the surge of tears. "Sometimes I wish I would have had the guts to let you try."

"I'm ready to try now. When we get Connor back.

That was the reason I called you about Shop with a Cop. I wanted to see you again. Find out if there could still be something there."

She wanted to reach out, to hug him. She longed to lean across the gulf between them and kiss him. But longing it or not, she couldn't take that kind of leap. Not when she didn't know what tomorrow would bring.

She crossed her arms over her chest.

"Megan?"

She wanted to say it wasn't him, it was her. But she couldn't throw that kind of easy answer at Ty. He deserved more. He deserved the truth. She just wasn't sure what that was. "I'm trying."

He brought his hand to her face and wiped tears from her cheek she hadn't even known she'd shed. "What can I do to change things?"

It was only a wisp of a touch, but one she could feel reverberate through her whole body. "I wish I knew."

Chapter Eight

The grand total of snow had reached seventeen inches, but even though the street outside Ty's house wasn't a main artery, it was still largely cleared before noon.

Ty had spent the morning on the phone. He'd called most of the businesses on Keating's client list, asking basic questions, trying to get a feel for each place, attempting to determine if it had anything to steal that was worth risking a kidnapping charge. Those where potential profit didn't seem to warrant such a risk, he crossed off the list. He ended up deleting a lot of names, and when finished, he was left with the pharmaceutical company, the jewelry store and two places that hadn't answered their phones.

With Megan's help, he blew snow off the driveway and shoveled the steps clear. And they were just about to head out and dig out his car when his phone rang.

Ty stared at the number on the caller ID. He'd figured Leo would call sooner or later. He wished he knew what his lieutenant wanted before he picked up. He'd love to get the news that the chief had reconsidered and his suspension was over before it really began. He needed to know whether they'd discovered Doug's lie about having Connor. But he anticipated the call would be neither of those things. If he was a betting man, he'd wager Leo wanted to grill him about the incident at Keating Security last night.

And that was a phone call Ty didn't want to take.

"Are you going to answer?" Megan asked. She cradled her fourth cup of coffee in her palms and was jumpy enough to have consumed eight.

Not that Ty could blame her. She'd been through hell yesterday and hadn't slept much last night. He'd heard her moving around in the spare room through the paper-thin walls. More than once he'd detected a sniffle, as if she was crying. He'd wanted to knock on her door, offer her what comfort he could give. But he knew she wouldn't accept it any more than she had earlier in the night. "It's Leo's cell. I think I'll pass."

The ringing stopped.

"I'm sorry for dragging you into that mess last night. I don't think I ever actually said that."

He shook his head. He could follow with another apology for losing Connor, but he wished instead that they could just stop this sorry game. "We're in this together, Megan. Right?"

She nodded. But the gesture did nothing to alleviate his concerns.

After digging out Ty's car, they tucked Megan's in his garage out of the sight of the kidnapper. If he really was watching her apartment, he might be keeping an eye out for her vehicle, as well. They couldn't risk him spotting Ty in Megan's car.

Megan pulled one of Ty's Green Bay Packer stocking caps over her head. With that and her sunglasses and parka, she blended in with half the people in town. The two of them ventured out into the snowy streets to the first business remaining on their list.

One of the businesses that hadn't answered the phone this morning turned out to be a pawn shop. The doors were barred, the place having been put out of business, apparently. How a pawn shop of all places had managed to go out of business in this shaky economy, Ty hadn't a clue.

Their second stop was the pharmaceutical company. Just from one glance he could see the place had security that could rival the White House. They didn't get past the front door, and even the employees had to go through intensive security, judging from the look of things.

They climbed back into the car and set off for downtown.

Megan stared straight ahead, clutching her bag in her lap with both hands, knuckles showing white.

"You okay?"

She glanced at him. The green in the hat and barely suppressed emotion made her eyes glisten like emeralds. "If whoever took Connor is planning to break into that place…" She shook her head as if she was totally at a loss. "Why didn't they just get the codes from Keating themselves? Keating's own security isn't that tough."

He'd had the same thought. Only skilled professionals could get past the myriad cameras and scanners they'd seen at Ellenston Pharmaceuticals, even if they had the codes. "It is probably not the target."

She didn't look relieved. "So we cross it off the list?"

Just as he was about to suggest he talk to someone at the department to see if there was any reason not to, his phone rang. He pulled it from his belt and glanced at the readout. Clipping it back in place, he continued to drive.

"Your lieutenant again?"

"Yeah."

"Maybe something happened. Something important."

"If he wants to tell me something, he can leave a voice mail. Otherwise I'm not ready to put myself up for questions. Not without knowing what I'm getting into."

"You're afraid he's going to ask you about me?"

"I'm afraid he's going to *interrogate* me about you. Or Doug." He wondered if she knew how hard this was for him. He was a cop, had always been a cop, had always wanted to be a cop. To cover up the mess at Keating, to duck his lieutenant's calls…he felt like he was splitting himself in two.

He pulled the car to the curb not too far from the little jewelry store on Main Street. He had no idea if Megan remembered this place, but he did. It had changed hands since then. But every time he drove past it, he remembered the Christmas right before he left for the police academy. He'd splurged on what he thought was the most romantic gift ever given. The diamond bracelet Megan had refused to accept.

Sometimes it was hell living in the same town where you grew up.

Before exiting the car to head into the store, he un-clipped his phone. Sure enough, Leo had left a voice mail. Probably a warning that if he didn't come in, his suspension would go from bad to worse. "I'll be just a second."

Megan stared out the window as if thinking of some-thing far out of her reach.

He left the car running to power the heater, punched in his PIN and held the phone to his ear.

"Ty, call me as soon as you get this. We need to talk about what happened last night at Keating Security."

He knew it. The thought of explaining why he'd chucked everything he knew was right and covered up for Megan made his palms start to sweat.

"I also thought you should know the paper is doing a piece on you and the scare with the kid. You're not going to like this, but I've gotten word they're calling it 'Wannabe Santa Claus' to be cute. But the article is far from a feel good holiday fluff piece. Just wanted to warn you."

The only thing that stopped Ty from groaning was the fact that Megan would no doubt ask what had caused it. He would have to tell her the money for Connor's disas-trous Shop with a Cop outing had come from him, not the department. He cringed inwardly at the thought. He'd misrepresented the department, tricked her into taking gifts from him and lost her son in one efficient screwup. She would be about as happy with his brilliant idea as Leo and the chief had been.

She'd probably hate him.

Resisting the urge to glance at her, he put the cell

away and turned off the ignition. He'd tell her. Just as he would come clean with Leo.

Eventually.

Right now he had to focus on finding out who might have taken Connor. And even though this fishing expedition they were on was far from efficient, until he could convince Megan to go to the police, this was all he had.

"That bad, huh?"

He pulled the key from the ignition. She'd obviously read his expression. He'd have to be more careful. "Let's go."

They climbed from the car and entered Radiant Diamonds.

The place looked much as it had when he'd bought that bracelet five years ago. Glass cases stretched from one end of the place to the other, and the shelves inside each were filled with sparkle. Diamonds and other precious stones, handmade jewelry using what looked like precious and semiprecious stones and spun glass caught every ray of sunlight streaming in from the window and reflecting on the snow outside.

He needed sunglasses, indoors or not.

They probably did a good business during tourist season, when Lake Hubbard was overrun with wealthy Chicagoans on vacation. And what's more, all he could see in terms of security was an alarm system with an internal motion sensor, much like the one Keating had installed in their own place of business.

"May I help you?"

Ty turned to see a squat, heavyset man who looked as brutal as a bulldog. "Ah, yes."

"Let me guess," he growled. "An engagement ring."

Megan said, "No, nothing like that," at precisely the same time as Ty said, "Yes, thanks."

Ty felt a familiar sinking in his chest. Even though he actually hadn't been going to buy Megan an engagement ring, it was as if the past rejection of that damn bracelet was playing itself all over again.

He needed to get his head together.

The man frowned. "So, you never asked or what?"

"Ah, we talked about it." They should have gotten their stories straight before they walked in the door. He hadn't realized they were in for an interrogation even in the damn jewelry store.

"Yeah. Briefly." Megan gave him a weak smile, trying to play along.

"And you didn't know why you were coming in here today?"

"I thought we were looking at necklaces for my mother," she said, voice hesitant.

"Why don't you look at both?" The man smiled. He pulled out a small ring of keys, moved to one of the cases and opened it so fast even the most timid shopper wouldn't have time to withdraw.

He also didn't have time to deactivate any additional security on the glass cases beyond the small lock on each. This place was nearly begging to be robbed.

The salesman started with a couple necklaces, but apparently picked up the feeling that Megan didn't really know what she wanted, so he shifted to the rings.

"Princess cut, square, and here's the most exquisite round diamond I have ever carried in this store. Platinum setting, too." He opened a small box.

Megan took in a sharp breath.

The man smiled. "Beautiful, isn't it?"

"Yes. It is, but..."

"Oh, you have to try it on."

Megan looked like she wanted to run from the store.

Ty felt a little queasy.

The man grinned. "Sometimes it helps to see it on your hand before you know whether or not you're ready."

"Try it on," Ty said. They'd seen what they needed to see, as far as the security, or lack thereof, was concerned. The quicker they played along with the rest of this, the sooner they could check out the next place on their list.

Megan sighed and held out her hand.

The jeweler slipped it on her finger. "Perfect. I don't think it even has to be sized. Now hold it up. Take a good look."

Ty leaned close. He didn't have much of an eye for jewelry. It all just looked like sparkly stuff, as far as he was concerned. But he had to admit, the ring was beautiful on Megan's hand. Almost like it belonged there.

"No. I don't think so." Megan pulled the ring off and handed it back. "It's too expensive."

"I have a full range of prices. Let's see what else..."

"No. I mean, thank you, but I...I don't think I'm ready for something like that."

"I guess we have some things to work out first." An

understatement if Ty had ever uttered one. They were here to take a look at the security, not rings. And there, he reminded himself, they had scored big time. "Thanks for your time."

"Why don't the two of you talk things over? We'll be here when you decide." The manager gave them a patronizing smile and handed both Ty and Megan a business card.

Apparently in case they wanted to shop alone next time. Ty returned the bulldog's phony grin. "Thanks."

He took one last look around. A burglary here would definitely be profitable. Maybe a little risky, being on the main drag, but all in all a much easier target than the pharmaceutical company and more profitable than stealing artisan cheese.

And the whole charade with the ring? The fact that Megan couldn't even pretend to accept a diamond from him shouldn't surprise him. After the would-be Santa Claus article came out, he doubted she'd be willing to accept anything from him again.

He held the door open for her, something he knew she hated.

As they stepped back out onto the snowy sidewalk, Megan glanced up at him. "I'm sorry."

"For what?"

"For not playing along better in there. I'm not very good at lying."

He knew he shouldn't feel so hurt by her choice of words, but he couldn't help it. "Wanting to get engaged to me is that big a lie, is it?"

She looked away from him and focused on his car

alongside the curb up ahead. Her steps quickened. "That's not what I meant."

He shook his head. He was such a jerk. Really, he shouldn't be surprised at her reaction. The way he was behaving, who would want to even pretend to be his fiancée? "Listen, I'm sorry."

She kept walking.

He hit a button on his remote and unlocked the car doors. Quickening his pace, he pulled beside her. This whole situation, seeing her again, being close to her, had dug up all of his insecurities. He needed to explain himself. "It's just that…I've bought you jewelry before, and you refused it. I'm a little sensitive about the issue. Even if this time it wasn't real."

"Jewelry?"

Now he wanted to crawl under the nearest snowdrift. Good thing there were plenty around. "The diamond bracelet."

"You gave me the bracelet after you told me you were leaving, Ty. It wasn't the gift, it was the timing. I didn't need a pity gift or an apology gift or whatever you intended it to be."

"I just wanted to give you something that you could look at every day I was gone. So you could remember me." The explanation sounded selfish, even to his own ears.

"Even though you left, you wanted me to wait for you. You wanted to know I'd still be there."

That was it. And now, understanding that, he could see why she'd given it back. He couldn't blame her one bit.

She reached for the door handle. Something fluttered

out of her hand and rested on a pile of snow along the curb. She picked up the card, then stared up at him, eyes wide.

"What is it?"

She handed him the business card the jewelry store owner had given her. "His name. Valducci. I think his family is tied to the Chicago mob."

Chapter Nine

Megan wished she hadn't said anything. Not until she was sure. But the sight of that familiar name on the business card coupled with their discussion last night had her mind racing.

Ty blew out through tense lips, his breath fogging in the air.

His brows pulled low. "How do you know this?"

"Through Doug." Megan didn't want to go into those days in Chicago when her life fell apart for a second time. She didn't even want to think about them. But if she knew Ty, she was going to have to tell him what she knew, difficult as it was. He wouldn't leave her alone about it until she did.

She glanced around at the quaint shops and restaurants of Lake Hubbard. The place was quiet compared to tourist season, but that only made her feel more exposed. She shivered. "Can we sit in the car or something?"

Ty opened her door.

She settled into the passenger seat. Even though they'd only been inside the jewelry store for a short time, the air in the car felt colder than outside. And as still as the inside of a freezer. She shivered again.

Ty slid into the driver's seat. Saying nothing, he started the engine and switched the heater to high, his unspoken questions hovering between them.

"Doug has a gambling problem. Sports, mostly. It started out as something social, and he ended up really getting into debt."

"In debt to the Valducci family?"

She shrugged. "I don't know if they're related. But the name doesn't seem too common."

"Is that why he embezzled money from your clients? To pay off gambling debts?"

She had wanted to think Ty didn't know about the embezzlement. She should have figured he did. Word certainly did travel fast in their hometown. And it often arrived embellished. "Then you know."

"Why you lost your investment business? Why you have to settle for cleaning jobs?" He nodded. "My aunt Sheila keeps me up on everything. You should know that."

Megan smiled. Sheila had been one of her favorites of all Ty's family. She knew everyone's business, but she was never malicious. And she was quite a matchmaker.

"You shouldn't have had to pay for what he did."

She let the smile drop from her lips and shrugged her coat tighter around her. Warm air blasted from the vents, but Megan wondered if she'd ever get warm.

Her life had been turned upside down after Doug's arrest. For a time, the police had even believed she was part of his scheme, and he had let them think it. In fact, he'd tried to blame the whole thing on her. But as painful as it was that Ty knew about those dark times, it was reassuring in a way, too. It made her feel less alone.

And that in itself should probably have her worried.

She focused her thoughts on her ex-husband. "Do you think it's possible that Connor was kidnapped because Doug couldn't pay off his debt?"

"Maybe. But if that's the case, why didn't they contact him after Connor was taken? Why call you?"

She didn't have an answer. Or maybe she did. "Because I'm the one who had the job cleaning Keating Security. And I was supposed to have the expertise to get the security files." Too bad she hadn't actually had that expertise. Too bad she'd failed.

"Did Doug get a call at all?"

"Not that he told me. Unless the kidnapper called him since we last spoke."

"If the Valducci family is behind this, why would they target their own store?"

"To collect insurance money?"

Ty arched his brows. "Insurance fraud. Yeah. That could be possible. The store certainly isn't a very hard target. And if they could blame the theft on you, or better, Doug, who has a record…I can see it."

"So how do we find out more about something like that? It's not like we can ask the Valducci family."

"You're not going to like my answer."

She felt a sinking feeling in the pit of her stomach. "The police department."

He held up a hand as if to stay her protests. "I can talk

to some people. See what they know. We don't have to make this official."

"And they won't try to find out why you're asking about the mob's connection to this jewelry store?"

He shrugged a shoulder.

"You can't tell them why, Ty."

"I won't. Trust me."

She pressed her lips together and pulled her coat tighter. She stared out the window at the snowy street. She did trust Ty. She wanted to.

Ty brought a hand to her jaw. He'd pulled off his glove, and his fingers were warm on her skin. He turned her to face him, his eyes searching hers. "We're in this together, Meg. We need to work together, to trust each other."

For a moment, she thought he would kiss her, and she couldn't remember wanting a kiss so much. At least not since she was twenty and still believed in love.

She pulled in a shaky breath and dropped her gaze. He was right. If they were going to find Connor, they had to work together. And they also had to each use whatever resources were at their disposal. And Ty wasn't the only one who had them. "I take it you don't want me with you."

"In this case, it would make things a little harder to explain."

"Okay. Find out what you can. We can meet in an hour at the next place on our list."

He pulled the printout from his coat pocket and took a glance. "Julianne's is the only one left. It's at 533 Lake Drive."

She nodded, recognizing the name of one of the places

she had never heard of before, and one that hadn't answered its phone this morning. "Julianne's."

She just hoped that when she next saw Ty, neither one of them had made a horrible mistake.

A FEW OF THE DETECTIVES AT THE Lake Hubbard P.D. were creatures of habit. Every day, workload willing, they would venture out of their offices, cross the street, amble down the block and duck into a place called Buck's for lunch.

The scent of hot hamburgers and stale beer hit Ty as he pushed his way into the bar. Sports memorabilia and television sets tuned to hockey, basketball and NFL prognostication covered every corner, pushing the decor and the sound level into the loud range. But despite the noise, the place wasn't busy.

In fact, it was downright dead.

Ty glanced in one booth after the next, expecting to see at least one detective chowing down a Buck's Behemoth with cheese, a side of pepper fries and a Coke. But there wasn't a cop in the place. He leaned against the bar and cleared his throat to get the bartender's attention.

A skinny kid wearing an orange Buck's T-shirt threw aside the bar towel he was using to wipe down bottles and turned to Ty with a smile. "Here for the lunch order, officer?"

"Lunch order?"

"Six Behemoths, fries, soda to go?"

"Sorry. Is that order for the P.D.?"

"Yep."

No wonder the place was void of cops. They were

ordering in today. He wondered why. "What time did you give for pick up?"

The kid glanced at his watch. "Less than five minutes from now. That's why I thought you must be here for it."

Five minutes. Only one detective would make the pick up. And he'd be able to ask that detective a few questions without others looking on and asking questions of their own. And without risking a run-in with Leo, or worse the chief.

Five minutes hadn't yet passed when Todd Baker pushed through the door and bellied up to the bar.

"Hey, Baker." Ty slid onto the bar stool beside him. "You piss people off or something? Where is everybody?"

"Big case. A shooting out in Lake Pass."

A solidly working-class neighborhood of tiny ranch houses and no lakefront to speak of, Lake Pass was a quiet area with little drama. A shooting was unusual for Lake Hubbard. It was downright bizarre in Lake Pass. "Dead?"

"As a doornail."

"What kind of shooting?"

"Looks like suicide. But there are a few loose ends we've got to tie up before we're making any kind of announcement." He flagged down the bartender with a wave of his hand.

The kid plopped three liter bottles of cola in a bag, set it on the bar, and disappeared through the swinging door leading into the kitchen.

Baker pulled out his wallet and fished out a stack

of bills. "Word has it you've been busy since I saw you yesterday."

Ty tried his best innocent look. Had Baker or someone else followed up with Doug yet? Was he fishing for information? Hard to say. "What do you mean?"

"Talked to Ed. He told me you're moonlighting as a janitor now."

He should have guessed that would come up. Ed had a love for gossip that rivaled a teenage girl's. "Not exactly. I was just helping a friend."

"A friend, eh? Figured. I also heard you and Megan Garvey had a thing at one time."

"Sounds like you've been hearing a lot of things lately."

"Helps to know how to listen." Baker thumbed through the cash in his hand and laid some bills on the bar.

Ty wasn't sure he wanted Baker to listen too hard to what he was about to ask. The detective was a smart guy. The last thing Ty wanted was him putting the pieces together.

No, the last thing Ty wanted was to fail to figure out who had Connor until it was too late. "Know the name Valducci?"

"Owns the jewelry store."

"So everyone knows who owns Radiant Diamonds except me?"

Baker shrugged. "Me and the missus bought our anniversary bands there. Diamonds in the bands. Got a good price." He held up his hand, flashing a sparkly ring.

It figured. And Ty had spent the past five years avoiding everything about the place…and the memories that went with it. "He's from the Chicago area, right? Marco Valducci?"

"What are you getting at, Ty?"

"Heard he was from a mob family. Is it true?"

"That surprises you? You're from around here. You know Lake Hubbard wouldn't be more than farm fields if not for the mob needing a summer getaway."

He nodded. When he was a teen, a lot of his friends had found those stories exciting. "Has Marco made any family members angry lately?"

Baker narrowed his eyes. "You'd have to ask the FBI that one."

"You haven't heard anything?"

"Nope."

"How about debt? His business hurting?"

"I wouldn't know."

"Know of any burglaries in the area? Not the usual. Something bigger."

"Heard there was one at Keating Security last night."

Ty forced himself not to tense up. "Ha ha. I'm serious."

"Why? You know something?"

"Not enough. Not nearly enough. But if I find out anything, you'll be the first I'll tell."

The kitchen door swung open and the bartender shuffled back behind the bar, four bags in his hands. He set them next to the soda in front of Baker and scooped up the cash. The aroma of grilled beef and fried food infused the air.

Ty took a deep breath, realizing neither he nor Megan

had eaten since early morning. "I'll let you get back to your delivery. And your shooting."

"Why don't you come with me? I know Leo was trying to get hold of you earlier."

"You wouldn't know why, would you?"

"Afraid not. But it has something to do with the media. They were crawling all over him, even before the report of the shooting came through. I think it's tied up with the kidnapping scare yesterday."

Ty nodded. Kidnapping scare. So thanks to the snowfall and the shooting in Lake Pass, the P.D. had yet to follow up with Doug. At least that much was going their way. So far.

"Other than that, I can't guess what those vultures are after." Baker opened a bag, fished out a pepper fry and popped it into his mouth. He tilted the bag toward Ty. "Want one?"

Ty held up a hand. "Tell Leo I'll give him a call as soon as I can."

"With all that's going on, Leo's a bit on edge." Baker threw a tip on the bar, stuffed the rest of his change in his pocket, and started for the door with his paper bags. "Your call better come soon."

MEGAN HADN'T STEPPED INSIDE Lake Hubbard's city hall since she and Doug had picked up their marriage license. In retrospect, it was not the happiest of memories, yet it was much happier than she was today.

She had no idea if what she was about to do would make her chances of getting Connor back better or worse. She just knew they weren't getting anywhere guessing which business was going to be targeted by the kidnapper. No matter what Ty said about checking information with the police and mob ties and whatever else, she felt like they were groping in the dark.

Time was running out. She had to try.

She did her best to push her doubts aside. Striding down the hall, she reached the mayor's office, opened the door and stepped inside.

"Hello. Can I help you?" A woman with bejeweled reading glasses propped on her nose gave her a reserved smile.

"Ah, yes. I was hoping I could have a word with Evan, I mean Mayor Blankenship."

The woman glanced down at her computer screen. "Well, he has a busy day, of course. I could set up something for you tomorrow."

"I can't wait until tomorrow. Can't you squeeze me in somewhere? It's kind of important."

The smile dropped from the woman's lips. She peered over her glasses, as if sizing up Megan and assessing her worthiness. "And your name is?"

Megan gave the woman her name.

"And your address?"

"He knows my address. Please. This is urgent."

The woman tilted her chin downward and scrutinized Megan over the top of her glasses. "He knows your address?"

"We went to high school together. He just stopped over to my house yesterday. I assume he knows how he got there." She felt like a fraud, building up this largely exaggerated connection between them. But being truthful and polite and self-deprecating wasn't going to get her what she needed.

The woman's smile was back. "I can check with Mayor Blankenship, if you'll wait here. What shall I tell him this is about?"

Megan opened her mouth, but didn't have any words to push out. What did she tell the woman? *This is about my plot to steal security information? This is about saving my son's life, but don't tell the police?*

"Megan!" Evan Blankenship's voice boomed through the room.

She turned to see him standing in the doorway at the back of the reception area.

"Did you come to say hi?"

"Ah, yes." She gave the woman a glance.

She was already back to peering through her fancy glasses at her computer screen, as if she had forgotten the problem of Megan Garvey had ever existed.

"Come on in. I have a Christmas tree lighting at the mall in about a half an hour, but since our people have done such a bang-up job plowing the streets, I should still have a few moments to catch up." He gave her a wink and motioned her into the office.

Megan's legs felt suddenly heavy, but she forced them to carry her inside.

"Please, take a seat."

Evan's office wasn't large, but Megan had a sharp enough eye to notice the handsome grain to the sturdy oak desk, the beautiful numbered prints decorating the walls and the obvious quality of the buttery-looking leather covering the chairs. His office might be that of a public servant, but his furnishings must be paid for with Harris money.

She sat, the leather's scent and softness wrapping around her.

Instead of sitting behind his desk, Evan dragged another chair next to hers and sat so close their knees were almost touching. "I was so grateful to hear Doug had your son. What a relief."

Megan hoped her smile appeared genuine and that Evan didn't notice how her fingers were trembling. "Thank you. It was quite a scare."

"I can imagine. Dee Dee and I don't have children, but I shudder to envision what that kind of situation is like. I think it would make me desperate enough to do anything."

Megan clasped her fingers together to still them. "Yes. It was horrible."

"But all's well that ends well, right? Where is your son now?"

"He's still with Doug. They are planning to visit the children's museum." At least the lies were coming easier every time she told one, although she wasn't sure that was something to celebrate.

"Oh, that's nice."

Silence stretched awkwardly between them, as if they'd burned up every common thread in the span of thirty seconds. She tried to come up with some way of steering the conversation toward Keating. The mansion's security? Her job? It all seemed to beg questions. Questions she didn't want to answer.

Even glanced at his watch. "So what brings you here to see me today?"

Maybe Ty was right. Maybe she shouldn't be here. She couldn't tell Evan why she needed help. She couldn't even come up with what she really needed him to do. Maybe this whole thing was a horrible mistake. "You need to get to work."

He looked at her blankly.

"The Christmas tree lighting ceremony. I'm holding you up."

"Yes, work. I guess that is my work now. Funny." He let out a chuckle that seemed a little forced. "Now, where did you say you worked again, Megan? I forget."

"I don't think I ever said."

"Are you still in the computer business?"

"No. I'm working for...I was working for Doug's cousin Gary. He has an office cleaning business."

"Was?"

"I was let go yesterday."

"Yesterday? Really? That's horrible."

He had no idea. But miraculously, she had the opening she needed. "That's why I'm here, actually."

"I don't think we're hiring currently, but I can ask Karen to check with the rest of city government. Or maybe Dee Dee is looking for additional help around the house."

Megan's face heated. She held up her hands. "That's very generous of you, but I'm not looking for you to give me a job."

He looked a little relieved and a lot confused. "You said you were fired, and that's why you're here."

"Yes. But I was actually wondering if you might have a word with Mr. Keating."

"Keating? The owner of Keating Security?"

"I've heard he installed the new security system at Harris House. Or is it the Blankenship House now?"

He waved away the name. "It's Harris House. Dee Dee's family has such a history here, we aren't going to change it. She didn't even take the name Blankenship. I don't blame her, of course. It's very long." His lips pulled back from straight white teeth.

Megan knew it was supposed to be a grin, but the expression looked so practiced, it made her even more uncomfortable. "Anyway, I was fired because I accidently set off the alarm while I was cleaning Keating Security last night. And I thought, maybe if you mentioned something to Keating, he might give me a second chance."

"And you're sure Gary Burke would hire you back if Keating gave his blessing?"

She had no clue. But it was the only idea she could come up with that might get her back inside Keating. "I'm sure of it. Gary has been good to me." At least that was the truth. All in all, he had been.

"Then consider it done. I'm sure Keating will do what he can to ensure he keeps Harris House on his client list."

Megan gave Evan a smile, an authentic one this time, and tried not to think of the fact that once she had the security information from Keating's computers, she would be turning over Harris House security codes to a kidnapper along with the rest. She might feel like a lying, pathetic sleaze at the moment, but getting Connor back was worth the price. "Thank you."

"Don't mention it. I'm sure you'd do me a favor if I needed one." He grinned, as if he had one in mind this minute.

"You bet."

"And come election time, I might just have to call in that favor." He added a chuckle to the grin, but Megan had the feeling he wasn't kidding at all.

Chapter Ten

Megan had thought she was about as uncomfortable as she could get when she'd asked Evan Blankenship for a favor. She'd been wrong.

She stood frozen in the doorway of Julianne's, the chime still sounding in her ears. The outside of the shop had held no more clues to what kind of business went on inside than the listing at Keating Security. But the moment she stepped inside, she had no doubts.

A mannequin stood in front of the store modeling the latest in leather and chains, a whip in its hand. Erotic art covered the walls, hot and explicit enough to make her blush. Some kind of musk perfumed the air. And every shelf held some kind of phallic toy, fur-lined handcuffs or various clamps and devices that made Megan cringe.

And in the middle of all of it stood Ty, a grin on his face. "Glad you found the place."

"Funny. I don't think I am." She stepped inside and let the door close behind her. She took one step, then another. The deeper she ventured into the place, the more exotic the wares became. Finally she just riveted her gaze to Ty, although she wasn't convinced looking at him was safer.

He let out a laugh. "Isn't this place great? Not sure it should be on our list, but..."

"Hello," a feminine voice cooed from behind her. "Welcome to Julianne's House of Pleasure."

Megan turned around to find an older petite woman who looked like she'd be more likely to offer a cup of chamomile tea than pleasure of any kind.

The woman stepped out of an office located at the side of the store, a smile on her face. "What type of pleasure can I help the two of you with today?"

"Um, you don't actually..." She wanted to pull a bag straight over her head. And here she thought her face was hot in Evan Blankenship's office.

"Don't actually?" She raised her brows.

"Provide pleasure," Megan choked out.

The woman gestured to the displays around her. "I provide the tools. He'll have to give you the pleasure." She tossed Ty a wink.

He had the audacity to laugh.

Megan was no prude, but she sure felt like one in this place. "No, I think there's been a mistake. We didn't know..."

"Didn't know what?"

She glanced at Ty, but he just grinned, as if he was enjoying the whole situation and wasn't about to bail her out of it.

"I didn't know a place like this existed. At least not in a little town like Lake Hubbard."

The woman seemed to find this amusing. "That's why

we don't advertise, dear. Those who want to come here know where it is. Those who find it bothersome don't. Everyone is happy, which is our aim, of course. Now can I help you with something to extend the pleasure he gives you, perhaps?"

Another chuckle from Ty.

She was going to slug him. "I'm sorry. We have to go." She grabbed Ty's arm.

He didn't move. "I was wondering, do you have other services?"

"What are you interested in?"

"Maybe in-home massage? You don't make house calls, do you?"

Megan stared at Ty. What was he doing? He gave her a wink, and she felt like slinking out the door.

The woman narrowed her eyes, as if sizing him up. "No, I'm sorry. We don't do anything like that. We just have the shop."

"I'm sorry to hear it." He stepped to the counter and took a business card from a holder on top of the cash register. He scribbled something on the back and handed it to the woman. "My phone number. In case you start offering more private services."

The woman took the card. "We'll see. In the mean-time, you might want to try some of the items here. You can also order online, if that makes you more comfortable."

Megan stuffed her hands into her pockets and looked from one to the other. Ty must be up to something. But until she knew what, she'd just have to play along.

He thanked the woman and gestured toward the door. "Shall we?" he asked Megan.

She nodded, glad to be leaving.

On the way out, Ty circled through the store. He paused near the office door and directed a pointed look at a security keypad next to another door, probably leading to the alley in back of the building. She followed him to the front of the shop, taking note of another alarm code pad next to the main entrance. Ty held the door open for her and stood to one side of the pad to avoid blocking her view.

The system was a simple one, more simple than the one at Keating Security. In fact, it looked as though only the doors were alarmed, no windows, no motion sensors. But that discovery did them little good. The place didn't hold anything valuable enough to justify kidnapping to get the alarm code.

They stepped outside. Crossing the street, they walked past a stand of evergreens to Ty's car, parked at the curb in front of a local snow-covered playground. The park backed up to the wrought iron fence of Harris House, and kids raced down the slope away from the fence on red and blue sleds, their happy shrieks piercing the air.

Megan swallowed a wave of emotion. She waited until they climbed back into Ty's car before she spoke. "Private services? What was that about?"

Ty raised his brows. "You mean, you're not interested in having an in-home massage?"

For a second, thoughts of Ty himself skimming his hands over her naked back flitted through her mind. She shook them away. "I'll pass."

"I was wondering why someone might want to break into a sex shop. What would a burglar steal that would be valuable enough to justify kidnapping?"

Just what she was thinking. "There's big black market demand for fur-lined handcuffs?"

He chuckled low in his throat. "Well, that might be. But I was thinking they might be doing something illegal behind the scenes."

"Prostitution."

He tilted his head, acknowledging that was exactly what he was thinking. "Or dealing drugs. Something that would mean they had money or something valuable like drugs in the store, something worth enough to go to great lengths to steal."

"And if there isn't anything like that?"

"Then we need to cross it off the list. But maybe we should take another look first."

She shot him a frown. She appreciated what he was doing, trying to lighten things up, especially since they seemed to be getting nowhere. But even Julianne's House of Pleasure and Ty's teasing couldn't loosen the knot in her stomach. In only a matter of hours the afternoon would draw to a close and evening would settle over the snowy town. The kidnapper could be calling at any moment, and they were no closer to knowing who he was or getting what he wanted. "What if there is no answer? What if we can't find it in time?"

"Then we'll figure out something else."

"What else?"

Ty shook his head, looking as lost as she felt. He stepped toward her and encircled her with his arms.

She should step back. Stand on her own. But she didn't have the strength for that anymore. No, that wasn't true. She didn't have the desire. God help her, she wanted Ty there with her. She wanted to lean on him. She wanted to hold him. She wanted him more than she'd wanted any man in a long time…any man since him.

She gave herself to his embrace.

She didn't know how long they stood there like that, and she didn't care. She could do nothing else. She'd fought her feelings for Ty for so long, ever since they were kids. She couldn't fight anymore.

A muffled ringing tone reached her ears.

Megan's heart jolted and started pumping double time. She pulled out of Ty's embrace and looked up at him.

Wordlessly, she unzipped her bag with a shaking hand and fished inside for her cell phone.

What if it was the kidnapper? What if he'd seen the two of them together? Or what if he'd seen her walking into city hall? She pulled the phone from her bag and looked at the readout.

Not the same number. A number she recognized. She punched the on button and held the phone to her ear. "Hello?"

"Megan. I'm glad I caught you."

She let out a shuddering breath. "Gary. I'm surprised to hear from you." She could feel Ty watching her, but she didn't meet his eyes.

"Believe me, I'm surprised to be calling. I got a call from Keating. Seems he's had a change of heart."

"A change of heart?" Megan could swear her own

heart was pounding so hard, Gary had to be able to hear it.

"Says he overreacted last night. He wants to give you a second chance."

So Evan had come through for her. The doubts he'd voiced about Gary flitted through her mind. "And you? Are you willing to give me a second chance, Gary?"

"I never wanted to fire you in the first place. You know that."

First Ty, then Evan, now Gary. If this kept up, she was going to turn into a regular believer in the goodness of men.

"Glad to have you back, Megan. But Keating's only willing to give you a two-hour window. Can you get it done in that amount of time?"

Two hours. That would be cutting it tight. But with Ty's help, she could do it. "Not a problem."

"Good. Now no more mistakes with the computers, eh? Don't let me down."

Her throat felt so thick she wasn't sure she could push out the lie. "I won't, Gary."

She punched the phone's off button and looked up at Ty. "I'm cleaning Keating tonight." And this time, she would be ready for the extra security. This time she'd get what the kidnapper wanted.

Furrows dug into his forehead. "How did that happen, exactly?"

"Mr. Keating had a change of heart."

"That's quite a turnaround. You don't look surprised."

Time to fess up. "While you were talking to your friends in the department, I made a visit of my own."

"To Keating?"

She didn't know why she felt so uneasy telling Ty, but she did. "To Evan Blankenship."

TY DIDN'T WANT TO ADMIT HOW much the fact that Megan had gone to Blankenship for help bothered him, but it did. He moved through the halls and offices of Keating Security, the backpack vacuum vibrating hot between his shoulder blades and roaring in his ears.

He'd spent last night struggling to convince Megan to accept his help getting Connor back, and yet she'd had no trouble waltzing into Blankenship's office this afternoon and asking him for assistance. He didn't know why he was surprised. Nothing had changed. Everything was just the same as when they were kids. Megan had turned down everything Ty had ever tried to give her, and yet as soon as he'd left for the police academy, she'd accepted Doug's ring.

So why did it still rattle him like a damn kick to the head?

He passed the office where Megan was hunched over the computer keyboard and moved on to the employee break room. They'd entered Keating Security as soon as the last employee left, and even with the days growing winter short, the sky had just fallen to darkness outside the office windows. Turning off the vac, he cleaned the microwave. Breathing in the scent of something recently cooked, he tried not to dwell on the fact that he'd missed lunch. He should have at least ordered a burger at Buck's when talking to Baker. Then he'd have gotten something valuable out of it.

He shoved his self-pity to the back of his mind. He didn't like covering for Megan again, but he had to remember why they were doing this. And if they could get Connor back safe, all the lying and breaking the law and denying every cop instinct he'd ever had would have paid off.

He wiped down the tables and counters, then fired up the vacuum and raked the wand over the tile floor. Stray crumbs vibrated as they shot up the aluminum tube. Reaching the dining area, he picked up chairs and flipped them seat down on the table so he could clean underneath.

A newspaper lay open on one of the chairs.

Ty let out a groan. The "Wannabe Santa Claus" story wasn't in this edition, but it would run tomorrow. He had to tell Megan the truth about the Shop with a Cop money before then. And when he did, what would she do? Ask Blankenship to help her the rest of the way? Rely on Doug to see her through this?

Leave him with a career in tatters and a truth he couldn't tell?

He shook his head. He'd made his own decisions, his own mess of his career. And as for him and Megan? None of that should bother him. He and Megan weren't a couple. She didn't owe him anything.

So why was this so hard for him? Why did her not being willing to play along at the jewelry store and the sex shop bother him so much? Why was the fact that she'd gone to Blankenship for help getting her back into Keating so hard for him to take?

The answer hung in the back of his mind, just as

it had for five long years. But now more than ever, he didn't want to look at it too closely. What was the point? Before tomorrow rolled around, he would have to find a way to tell her who had really financed the Shop with a Cop trip, and anything that might still be between them would be over for good.

He wadded up the newspaper and was about to toss it in the trash when a headline caught his eye. MALL SECURITY GUARD DEAD.

Chapter Eleven

Megan stared at the monitor. This couldn't be happening. This was her chance. Her last chance. It had to be here somewhere.

She glanced at her watch. Her two-hour window would be up soon. She and Ty would have to leave Keating Security or risk setting off the alarm again.

She scanned the directory once more, looking for hidden files. She must have missed something. The security files for each of Keating's clients couldn't have disappeared from their system. They had to be here.

As if she was going to suddenly discover them now. She'd been searching for almost two hours with no luck. It was as if the server had been wiped clean.

Not possible.

No doubt someone trained in computer forensics could retrieve the files. Unfortunately she didn't have that kind of training. The files were out of her reach.

And so was Connor.

She clapped her hand over her mouth, trying to force back the sob. What would happen to her little boy? Now that she couldn't come up with the files, what was she going to do?

She shut down the computer, backtracking, covering up her activities. She had to find Ty. She could only pray that he had an idea of what to do next.

Ty sat in the employee break room. The cleaning long since done and the equipment stowed away, he sat with a newspaper in his hands. He looked up from the newsprint. Lines dug into his forehead and bracketed his lips.

Probably a reflection of the stress on her own face. "I know why Keating agreed to let me come back."

He looked concerned, as if he'd already read her expression and knew what was coming was not good. "The files?"

"Gone. Wiped clean by someone more adept at this than I am." After her failure with the alarm and now this, she was beginning to think finding someone better at this wouldn't be hard. A wisp of hysterical laugher stuck in her throat. "I couldn't even come up with a client list this time."

"It's worse."

"Worse? How could any of this be worse?"

"You might want to sit down."

She teetered a little, her knees suddenly feeling weak. But she remained on her feet. "Tell me."

"The technician at the department store, the one who handled the surveillance cameras, the one who was on duty when Connor was abducted? He's dead."

"How do you know?"

Ty offered her the paper and pointed to a small article on the local page.

She scanned the headline. "You're sure it was the same guy?"

"Unless there's more than one tech named Derek working in security at the mall. It doesn't say much here, but Baker told me about the shooting this afternoon. He called it a probable suicide. He said they were waiting for the autopsy results and trying to tie up some loose ends before they made an announcement."

"What kind of loose ends?"

"I didn't know it was Derek Ernst, or I would have asked."

"So what does this mean?" She still wasn't putting together why the suicide of a mall security guard made her situation worse. "You said he was helping search for Connor yesterday at the store, but what does that have to do with getting Connor back now?"

"He was in charge of finding images of the kidnapper's face."

"Your lieutenant said there were no good images."

"Exactly."

The pieces shuffled into place in her mind. She was finally getting it. "You think he made sure there were no images to be found?"

"Maybe. There was also something peculiar about the kidnapper. Something I noticed in the footage I saw of him yesterday."

"What?"

"He never looked at the camera. He always turned so his face was hidden."

"You think he knew where the cameras were located?

"I think it's a pretty good bet."

She could see where his thoughts were leading. And she had wanted more than anything to grab whatever she could and call it a clue that would lead to Connor. But that didn't mean it was. Before she dared follow down the path Ty was going, she had to look at it from all angles. "Couldn't anyone spot security cameras if they took the time and knew what to look for? We can't be sure Ernst told him their location."

He tilted his head, conceding the point. "But I don't buy the coincidence. I have the feeling this is no suicide at all. And if that's true…"

"Derek Ernst was murdered." She finished his thought, the words hard on her tongue. "Why? To cover up a kidnapping?"

Ty's nod was nearly imperceptible. "He could have wanted a bigger cut of the profits. He could have been talking to police. Whatever it was, it's fair to say he was killed for a reason. And unless you believe in coincidence, odds are that reason has something to do with Connor's abduction."

"Is there any way we can find out more?"

"I can talk to Baker again. He's working on the case."

The familiar jitter started up again. She knew she could trust Ty. Didn't she? So why was she hesitating?

"Leo called again tonight. He didn't leave a message this time."

"You think he knows Doug doesn't have Connor?"

Ty didn't answer. But he didn't have to. The police wouldn't wait forever to follow up. Even if the snowstorm had slowed things down, they'd still have checked up on Connor by now. And if they knew Doug didn't have their son, they knew the kidnapper was still out there… somewhere…with her little boy. They would investigate. Exactly what the kidnapper ordered her to prevent.

But of course, she didn't have anything else the kidnapper wanted, either. "You still think I should go to the police."

"Of course."

She felt sick. He was probably right. What few options she had once had disappeared along with those security files. But she was afraid. If she did the wrong thing, made the wrong choice, it could cost Connor's life. She didn't know enough to make that kind of decision. She couldn't see enough of the situation. She was flying blind without any idea what danger would hit next. Without any sense of up or down. "What if the kidnapper finds out? What if it makes him angry? He said he'd cut his losses. He said he'd…"

"I don't think you understand, Meg." Ty's voice was quiet, but his tone was dead urgent. "If this kidnapper killed Ernst, that suggests he's covering his tracks."

"Covering his tracks? And Connor is one of those tracks he needs to make disappear?" She scraped her fingernails into the palms of her hands. She needed to move, to do something. Her head buzzed until she could barely think.

"I don't have to tell Baker everything. Not yet. Just enough to know what we're up against. To get some of the answers we need. Or at least to know how to find them ourselves. Will you trust me to do that?"

It wasn't a question of whether or not she could let herself rely on Ty. At this point, she didn't know what she'd do without him. "I trust you, Ty. With Connor. With everything."

DETECTIVE BAKER'S HOUSE LOOKED like so many other middle-class homes in the area. Split-level, with Christmas lights strung along the eaves and a wreath purchased from the Boy Scouts on the door. A decorated tree sparkled in the front picture window. The normalcy of the scene tightened in the back of Megan's throat with a longing she'd felt since she was a little girl. Houses like that were filled with family and love. They smelled like cookies baking and evergreen and sounded of laughter on Christmas morning.

She hadn't had much of that growing up. She hadn't known anyone who had until she met Ty. She'd sworn that's the kind of home she'd provide for her own son. A nice dream, and one that felt like it was fast fading away.

Ty passed it and pulled to the curb several houses down, just at the edge of a streetlight's glare. He seemed nervous about talking to Detective Baker, his fingers gripping and regripping the wheel. His tongue rubbed back and forth on his lower lip. On the entire drive from Keating Security to Baker's neighborhood, he'd been so focused, she doubted he'd even noticed her watching him in the glow of the dashboard.

And with each passing mile, she felt more awful.

He shifted into Park and twisted to face her. "I get the feeling you'd be pacing right now if the seat belt wasn't strapping you in."

Her mouth felt dry. She focused on the reflection in his eyes, their blue a light amid darkness. "I'm scared."

He nodded, not trying to talk her out of it, not trying to make her feel her fear was wrong in any way, just accepting it. Accepting her.

"Thank you."

"For what?"

"For being here for me."

"I think we've been through enough *thank you*s and *I'm sorry*s to last a lifetime, don't you?"

He was probably right. She didn't need to say anything, but she felt compelled to say it all the same. As if at any moment, everything could be over and she'd never have the opportunity to say another word. "You asked why I wouldn't accept anything from you. The help moving. The bracelet. Why I pushed you away."

"Yes?" He grasped her hand.

She couldn't feel his skin through both their gloves, but she drank in the pressure of his fingers like a woman dying of thirst. "The whole thing with my dad, it was really hard for me. When I found out he had a whole other life…" Her throat closed.

Ty squeezed her hand and waited for her to go on.

She swallowed hard and forced the words out. "It really shook me. And when my mom ended up in the hospital…" Again, she had to stop. She'd always known things weren't good between her parents. They'd never even pretended to have a happy life. But to know her father was living with another woman on the side, it nearly killed her mother. "I thought my dad was part of my family, then found out he really wasn't. I thought my mom was so strong, then when she tried to kill herself… it was like nothing I thought was true actually was."

"And you thought that you and I, what we had, that it wasn't true, either?"

She nodded, grateful that he'd said the words so she didn't have to.

"I think you were probably right about me not being ready to get married, to settle down. But I loved you, Megan. And the more time we spend together, the more I am beginning to think I still do."

She leaned toward him and he brought his lips to hers. His kiss was tender and gentle, although she could feel the passion built up behind it, as if he wasn't sure she was strong enough, what they had was strong enough, for him to let it loose. When the kiss ended, he looked into her eyes.

She had to tell him the rest. He had to know. "After you left, Doug was there."

He looked away, staring into the darkness outside the car.

"I didn't feel the same way about him. Never like I felt about you. And for some reason, that seemed safer to me. I thought if he disappointed me, it wouldn't hurt so much."

"So you married him."

"So I married him." And the rest was history, as they said. A sad history. "I wish I'd waited. I wish I would have been braver."

He brought his focus back to her. "And now? Are you braver now?"

She thought for a moment, even though she knew she could ponder hour after hour and still not know the answer. "I want to be."

He nodded, as if that was good enough. "We'll get Connor back. Maybe if you aren't using all your bravery for your son, you'll have some left over for me."

She gave him her best try at a smile. "I hope so."

Chapter Twelve

More than anything, Ty wanted to stay with Megan. To talk things out. Or maybe just be silent and hold her, maybe kiss her again. After she'd married Doug, he hadn't let himself think too much about what it would be like to get her back. How he would do things differently. But even though she hadn't totally opened that door, he felt that something major had changed between them. That there was hope. And with it, his whole life felt like it was shifting in front of him.

Not that either one of them could afford to spend time pondering those possibilities now. Not with Connor still out there. And although it was fairly early in the evening, they didn't have a moment to spare. When the kidnapper's next call came in, Ty wanted to know who they were up against. He wanted to know what their next move needed to be.

He took one last glance at Megan before he climbed out. "If anything happens, just drive."

"What's going to happen?"

"I don't know. Probably nothing." He'd been jumpy since he'd seen the story in the newspaper. He supposed a possible murder would do that. "But if something does, get out of here just the same. And if you can't for some reason, there's a gun in the glove box."

She glanced at the compartment in front of her with alarmed eyes. "I think I'll just drive."

"Probably best." He stepped out into the cold night, flicked the lock button on the car door and closed it behind him.

Baker answered the door wearing sweatpants and slippers. "Davis. What are you doing here?"

"Can I come in?"

The detective stepped to the side and motioned him inside.

The house smelled like baking cookies, and children's voices jabbered from the direction of a warmly lit kitchen. "Making sugar cookies. Want one?"

Normally Ty would make some quip about the fact that Baker happened to be baking, but not tonight. "No, thanks. Can we talk?"

Baker led him into the front room, barely big enough to house the giant Christmas tree dancing with lights that he'd noticed from the street. "What is it?"

"That shooting you mentioned yesterday. I read a little about it in the paper. You said it looked like suicide?"

"Yeah. Autopsy's scheduled for tomorrow." He narrowed his eyes on Ty, his stare every bit as piercing as Leo's. "What about it?"

"Derek Ernst. He was a security guard at the mall. A technician, worked on the security cameras."

"Yeah."

"He was there when Megan Garvey's son was kidnapped."

"Leo mentioned that."

"Don't you think that's strange? That he was working security when a kid was kidnapped in the morning and dead by nightfall?"

"I think he had a bad day."

"Or he was involved."

"Now you lost me, Ty. Ms. Garvey's ex-husband took the kid. She's fine with it. It's all over. There's nothing for Ernst to be involved in."

Apparently they still hadn't caught up to Doug. Ty bit the inside of his cheek. He wanted to tell Baker everything. He needed to. It would change the way he looked at his whole shooting case. But he'd promised Megan he wouldn't. At least not until he could convince her to give him the okay.

He reviewed the article's few details in his memory. "He was found in his car?"

Baker nodded. "About a half mile from his house out on Quarry Road. Shot himself in the head with an untraceable gun. Snowplow almost ran into him."

"An untraceable gun?"

"One of those loose ends. He has a gun registered to him, yet he used one he must have bought off the street."

"Have you taken a look around his house?"

"A little bit."

On the drive over, he'd even pondered the possibility that Ernst might have been keeping Connor. He wasn't sure how to ask Baker if there were signs of a little boy in the house without him wondering where the question had come from. "And?"

"No suicide note, if that's what you're asking."

"Anything else?"

"Nothing out of the ordinary."

Baker's vague answers weren't helpful at all. But what did he expect when he was limited to asking vague questions? "What kind of loose ends are you wrestling with?"

"You trying for a promotion to detective, Davis? Hate to put a damper on your ambitions, but from what I hear, you're not in great shape at the moment. The suspension. The media mess. 'Wannabe Santa.'"

So Baker had heard. It was only a matter of time before Megan did, too. He had to find a way to tell her. And soon.

Ty pushed the thought out of his mind for the moment and focused on the matter at hand. "Just give me an idea of what the case looks like. Maybe I can help. As you pointed out, I have a lot of extra time on my hands lately."

He got a smile out of Baker for that one. "Let's just say we're having trouble coming up with a reason for him to do it. Mother said he was happy. Got a raise recently. He dumped his high school girlfriend a little while back, a Corrine Blaska, but now he was going out with someone new. Leo says he seemed pretty full of himself yesterday in the security office."

Ty had to agree. Although he had trouble wrapping his mind around a guy like that having not one but two women interested in him. Sometimes there really was no justice. Of course, Ty had experienced that problem himself. It had been a lot of fun, but when it came down to anything more, he had only really been interested in one woman. "Mind if I take a look around Ernst's house? Maybe something will stand out."

Baker tilted his head to the side. "You've got to be kidding me."

"Like I said, I have a lot of time to fill. Sometimes a pair of fresh eyes makes a big difference."

Baker continued with the wary look. "You're serious?"

"It won't take long." Ty glanced at his watch, confirming it was still fairly early.

"You expect me to drive out there with you now?"

Ty shrugged a single shoulder in an attempt to look like he could take or leave the suggestion. "What? You worried it's past your bedtime?"

"I'm worried you're becoming a pain in the ass."

"Oh, come on, Baker."

"Clear it with the chief and Leo, and I'll be happy to show you around...*tomorrow*." Baker glanced back toward the kitchen where the voices and laughter were now mixed with the strains of Christmas music. "I gotta go."

Ty's mind raced. Ernst's death was the only break he and Megan had. He needed to follow it up. It was just a question of how far he was willing to go, and he already knew that answer. "Yeah, guess I'd better go, too."

Baker nailed him with another pointed stare. "Don't do anything stupid."

Ty tried to smooth all expression from his face. "I don't have a clue what you mean."

"You know, you're on thin ice after that Shop with a Cop thing you pulled."

How could he forget? "Don't worry about me."

"It's not you I'm worried about. It's my case, if there is a case."

"You have nothing to worry about then."

Baker looked at him out of the side of his eye. "Why is it that lately when you say *don't worry,* I feel the need to start worrying?"

"You're having sugar withdrawal?" Ty scooped the air in front of Baker with his hands, as if pushing him into the hall. "Now go back to your Christmas cookies. You're wasting away before my eyes."

"Daddy?" a voice called from the kitchen.

Baker let loose a heavy sigh. "Be there in a second."

He stepped out into the hall and led Ty to the front door. Yanking it open, he stood to the side to let him pass. "Don't touch anything."

"I don't know what you're talking about."

"I mean it. Not one thing."

"Yes, Dad. Merry Christmas."

IT WASN'T HARD FOR MEGAN TO spot exactly which Lake Pass home belonged to Derek Ernst. Christmas lights glowed red and green, blue and white, and every color of the rainbow on either side of the street, but for the house at 1498 Hillside. There, the only decoration visible was yellow police tape stretched across the span of the garage door and barring the front entrance.

Ty parked the car down the block, and he and Megan walked back to the scene. The night was quiet in a certain kind of hush only a thick blanket of snow could produce. The moon hung fat and round in the sky, making the snow glow blue, almost bright as day. Ice crunched under their boots.

They hiked around to the side of the house, the fresh, knee-deep snow sucking at their boots. Megan could feel it slip inside, packing cold around her calf and ankle until her skin was numb. She shivered, and her breath fogged in the air.

Ty paused beside the garage window and peered inside. Megan craned her neck, trying to see. The pane was filthy with spider droppings and cobwebs. Beyond that, all she could make out was darkness.

Ty glanced at Megan. "Garage window locks are often terrible, especially on old windows like these."

"You're going to break in?"

"I'm going to try."

A tremor started up in her chest at the thought. God, she was bad at criminal type stuff. "You're sure?"

"This from a woman who tried to steal files from a security company?"

"You have a point."

"Just don't touch anything. I promised." He thumped the heel of his hand against the frame of the top sash. "As long as the window isn't painted shut, it can be pretty easy." He slid the bottom sash up.

Megan nodded and made note that if she ever could afford a house again, she would install new locks on all garage windows.

Ty scanned the window frame for a moment before turning back to Megan once again. "I don't think I can fit. If I boost you through, you can let me in the back door." He leaned down and cupped his hands in front of her.

She stepped into his palms and gripped the window's edge. Ducking, she let him boost her inside. Sticky spiderwebs clung to her cheeks and hat. A cluster of round little egg sacs dangled in front of her eyes.

She lowered herself down to the concrete floor and did her best to wipe off the debris. At least it was winter. No spiders or other creepy crawlies would be alive this time of year. She could take comfort in that.

The garage was piled with boxes on one end, a collection of old yard equipment that looked like it hadn't seen use in eons and a car-sized space in the middle. The place smelled like old motor oil. Kitty litter crunched under her boots.

She shuffled to a door she hoped would lead inside, half feeling her way in the darkness. The knob turned under her hand, and she stepped onto a vinyl floor.

The house itself smelled musty, as if it hadn't gotten a good cleaning in a long while. Megan stifled the urge to sneeze. The back door. Where was it?

She wished she could turn on a light, but she didn't dare. She tiptoed through a kitchen in desperate need of cleaning, let alone complete renovation. Moonlight streamed through a sliding patio door on the other side of a pass-through counter. A wide-shouldered shadow blocked the span of glass. She unlocked the door and slid it wide.

Ty knocked the snow off his boots and stepped inside.

"Where do we start?" Megan asked, peering down a narrow and dark hall.

"Why are you whispering?"

"I don't know. I guess because we're not supposed to be here." She kept her voice low despite his teasing. She was uncomfortable with this whole situation. She just hoped it didn't end as badly as her criminal exploits at Keating Security had. "What are we looking for?"

"I have no idea. I'm hoping we'll know it when we see it. But if anything looks familiar to you, speak up. Any connection to Connor. Any connection to anyone you know."

Okay. She could do that. She turned away from the window and they headed into the dark house.

Not eager to face the long, dark hall, Megan ducked into the living room first. Moonlight streamed through the window, making the room so bright she didn't need to switch on the light. A single strand of twinkle lights was strung over the top of the picture window peering out at the street. The room was nearly empty except for an old couch, a lamp and a flat screen TV.

"Derek Ernst certainly lived like a bachelor," Ty noted.

Megan had to agree. Not that all bachelors lived that way. Ty was a bachelor, too. But Ernst's house was far from the warm, masculine surroundings of Ty's. This place held the bare, aimless look of a man who had yet to figure out who he was. Maybe the rest of his personality was packed away in the boxes she'd seen in the garage. "This place doesn't look like a girlfriend is around much."

"Maybe they hang out at her place."

She supposed it was possible. No woman in her right mind would want to spend much time here.

That impression was only strengthened by a look at the first bedroom. A queen bed dominated the space, a mattress, box spring and plain metal frame. The sheets and blankets were twisted in a lump on the mattress. An orange crate lay on its side next to the bed, an alarm clock balanced on top.

Megan couldn't imagine a woman in this room, either. "You sure he has a new girlfriend?"

Ty shrugged. "I have to say, I can't see anything that says he committed suicide, but I don't see any reason for him not to, either."

The next bedroom was a stark contrast to the rest of the house. Even in the light from outside, Megan knew they'd finally found the room in which Derek Ernst spent his time. "May the real Derek Ernst please stand up."

Ty switched on the light. The room smelled clean, the furniture dust free and carpet vacuumed so recently, it still held tracks. Movie posters covered the walls, their subjects running the gamut from *Star Trek* to *Star Wars*. A computer desk stretched along one wall, filled with cutting-edge hardware.

Ty nodded. "This is the guy I met in the mall, all right."

Megan gave the computer a once-over. It was running, the monitor merely in sleep mode. "Does touching something include bumping that mouse?"

"Pull on your gloves."

She did. The monitor flicked on. A photograph of a naked woman smiled from the screen.

Ty leaned toward the monitor. His eyes narrowed on the woman, but they didn't hold sexual interest. He looked more as though he'd seen a ghost.

Megan held her breath. "What is it?"

He glanced up from the photo and focused on Megan, his eyes intense as a cloudless sky. "I know her."

"You…how?"

He was about to answer when a faint voice trembled from the hall. "Who are you? And what are you doing here?"

Chapter Thirteen

Tiny and with the straight up and down body of a boy, the woman standing in the doorway to Derek Ernst's home office looked about as threatening as a wisp of cloud.

Until Megan focused on her eyes.

They glistened, each iris nearly as black as the pupil. Red rimmed, and intense enough to be lethal.

Or crazy.

The woman raised her hand. In her fist, she held a gun. "Who are you? What are you doing to Derek's things?"

Megan's throat went dry. Her pulse thundered in her ears. Here she'd been afraid the police would find them. That Ty would get in trouble. It had never occurred to her that they might be walking into real danger of the life-threatening kind.

"Put the gun down, ma'am." Ty's voice rang steady and commanding.

"Who are you?"

"I'm Officer Ty Davis. This is Megan Garvey."

She stared at them. Her gun hand started to shake, the barrel bobbing. "Officer? You're police?"

"I am. Now put the gun down."

"You're here…why? Did you find out more about Derek?"

"I know you've had a rough day. I'm sorry for your loss. But things are only going to get worse unless you set the gun on the floor. Now."

The woman looked at her hand. Her eyes grew wide, as if she was shocked to see what her fingers held.

"Set it on the floor."

Tears stuck in her lashes and spilled down her cheeks. She folded into a crouch and set the weapon on the carpet. Slowly she opened her fingers, as if she half expected the thing to scamper away.

"Stand up now. Leave it there."

She did. Her shoulders started to shake, like a volcano of sobs about to explode.

Megan knew the feeling. Her whole body quaked. Now that the gun lay harmless on the floor, her knees wanted to buckle. She pressed her thigh against the desk, bracing herself.

Ty closed in on the gun. "Take a step backward, into the hall."

As the woman retreated, Ty knelt down and picked up the weapon. He hit a button and a cartridge slid out of the handle. He pulled the top of the gun back, looked inside, then gave the barrel a sweep with his finger, as if making sure he could trust his eyes. "Unloaded."

"I…I didn't want to hurt anybody."

"Did it occur to you that you might be more likely to get shot if you go around pointing a gun at people? Whether the damn thing is loaded or not?"

"I didn't know you were a cop." Tears coursed down her cheeks. Judging from the red rims of her eyes, this wasn't the first time in the past few hours.

Megan doubted anything Ty was saying was getting through to the woman at all. At least she didn't seem crazy. She seemed broken.

"Where did you get the gun?" Ty asked.

She stared at him for a second, as if she had no idea what he was talking about.

"The gun," he repeated. "Whose is it? Yours?"

Finally the woman shook her head. "It's Derek's. It was in the closet."

"Derek's?" Ty's brows shot upward. "Does he have several guns?"

She shook her head. "Just one."

Megan tried to remember what Ty had told her about Derek Ernst's death and what she'd read in the newspaper. She was pretty sure Derek shot himself. Was it with his own gun? She thought so.

She looked up at Ty. "So whose gun is this?"

"It's Derek's," the woman said again.

"You're sure about that?"

She squinted at the weapon in Ty's gloved hand. "I... It looks like his gun."

"Are you...friends with Mr. Ernst?" Ty asked.

The woman nodded. "I'm his girl...I mean, *was* his girlfriend. We...we broke up."

"You and he were high school sweethearts?" Ty prodded. "You're Corrine?"

"Yes."

Ty nodded.

Baker must have mentioned the girlfriend's name, although Ty hadn't mentioned it to Megan. "If the two of you broke up, why exactly are you here?"

She held up a fob. A single silver key reflected the overhead light. "He gave it to me. He never asked for it back."

Ty gave her a tell-the-truth look that Megan could swear cops must practice in their bathroom mirrors.

"Okay, I had it copied." Corrine stuffed the key chain back in her pocket and swiped at her cheeks with the backs of trembling hands. "But I didn't use it before tonight. I swear. I had to come here. That's all. I just…"

"You wanted to feel close to him?" Megan supplied.

Corrine nodded.

Ty shot Megan a look clearly asking her to stop providing answers.

She pressed her lips together. She couldn't help it. Now that her panic at the sight of the gun had begun to subside, she was starting to feel sorry for the woman.

"When did you get here?"

"I don't know. After work, I guess."

"You were here when we arrived?"

"I must have fallen asleep. I woke up and noticed a light in here. So I found Derek's gun in his closet. I thought someone knew he was gone. I thought you were going to steal his computer or something. Not that it would matter now, I guess."

Ty stepped to the side and gestured to the computer screen. "Corrine, do you know this woman?"

She took a few more swipes at her eyes, then squinted at the computer. "Oh, her."

"You know her?" Megan asked. She looked from Corrine to Ty. It seemed she was the only one here who had never met the nude bombshell.

"Know her?" Corrine said, bringing Megan's focus back to her. "Not really."

"But you know her name," Ty said. "Don't you? And you know why she's on Derek's computer."

"Samantha. Samantha Vickery."

"He was dating her, wasn't he?" Ty prodded.

Corrine glanced to the side. "She just showed up in the mall one day all flirty, and that was it. The next thing I knew, Derek was saying he wanted to date other people. Other people, can you imagine? Like it could be anyone. Like I didn't know exactly who he wanted to date. All I've done for him, all we shared, none of it meant anything."

Furrows dug into Ty's forehead. "You said she showed up in the mall? Are you saying he met her by chance?"

"Yeah. I guess. I don't know. Come to think of it, she probably planned it. Yeah, I'm sure she did."

"When did this happen?"

"About a week ago."

"At the mall."

"Yes. We were having lunch in the food court and she just walked right up to our table and sat down. She was wearing this low cut blouse and kept leaning forward and touching Derek's leg. That was the last time he looked at me." She glanced at the computer screen. "Now I guess I know why."

Megan shook her head. Corrine's story sounded bizarre. Who just walked up to a couple and stole away the boyfriend? And how in the world did Ty know her? She caught his blue gaze. "Who is this woman?"

"Apparently, she's Samantha Vickery."

"But you said you know her. How do you know her?" She probably sounded like a jealous girlfriend herself, but she didn't care. Although she did feel some pangs, she had to admit, logically she knew there was a big difference between Ty and Derek Ernst. For Ty, she had a feeling there was more to his interest in this woman than sex. And that it had nothing to do with feelings and everything to do with Connor's abduction. "Who is she?"

"I only saw her once. In the mall. The day Connor disappeared."

Megan sucked in a breath. "She's involved, too?"

"She called herself the Giftinator. Walked up to me out of the blue and started talking about buying Christmas gifts. She distracted me. Just for a few seconds, but those were the same seconds when Connor was taken."

TY COULDN'T BELIEVE HE'D BEEN so damn stupid. Here he'd thought the Giftinator—*Samantha Vickery*—had been a random, somewhat annoying woman with nothing better to do than babble on about helping people buy gifts. He was a cop, for God's sake. He should have suspected something was up, shouldn't he? He should have tied her together with Connor's kidnapping from the first. Instead, in all the panic following Connor's disappearance, he'd simply wiped her from his mind.

He focused on Corrine Blaska. If anyone could

tell him more about the new girlfriend, it was the old girlfriend. "Where does Samantha Vickery live?"

Corrine stepped back, as if she wanted to fade into the hallway.

Maybe he was coming on a little strong. The woman was clearly on the edge of a complete breakdown. But they'd finally gotten a lead on Connor's kidnappers, and he didn't want to waste a single second.

He took a deep breath. Better to give Corrine a little motivation to help. "She stole your boyfriend. And she might have done a lot worse. I need to know everything you do."

"She lives on the lake. Right on the water. She took Derek there." She studied her boots. "I followed them."

"Where on the lake?"

"On the Eastern Shore. A fancy house with pillars in the front. It has a pool. It's right on the lake, and yet it still has a pool." She shook her head at the absurdity of it.

Ty knew the neighborhood. That whole area was built up by mob money in the bootlegging days. He couldn't wait to find out who was paying the mortgage. Just a guess, but he'd bet it wasn't Samantha Vickery. "Have you talked to the police about all this, Corrine?"

"About Derek? Why he would kill himself?"

"About Samantha Vickery."

She shook her head. "They didn't ask about her."

Not surprising. If Baker or Leo saw Samantha's nude photo on Derek's computer wallpaper, they'd probably assume he'd downloaded it from some internet porn website. As for the connection to Connor's abduction, Leo and Baker didn't even know the boy was gone until… come to think of it, Baker hadn't mentioned Connor at all. How was it possible they still didn't know?

"We have to go." Ty exchanged looks with Megan, then focused on Corrine. "Are you going to be okay? Do you want us to drop you off somewhere?"

"I'll be fine." She looked past him, focusing intense eyes on the computer monitor.

Great. The last thing he wanted was for her to erase the photo or something. "We'll take you home."

"That's okay. I have my car here."

"But you're in no shape to drive. And on the way, you can point out the house where Samantha Vickery took Derek."

"It's not on the way to my apartment."

"Oh, yes, it is. We're taking the long way."

MEGAN LOOKED UP AT THE BIG white house on the lake that could have swallowed her entire apartment building and had room left over for dessert. Her head had been buzzing since Corrine had first pointed out the house. The time it had taken to drop her off at home and return had seemed to stretch on forever. Could Samantha Vickery know where Connor was? Could she have him in that house right now? Could he be locked in a room? Scared? Needing his mommy?

She glanced at Ty. She knew he'd wanted to call in the police since the moment he saw the woman he'd known as the Giftinator on Derek Ernst's computer screen. No, who was she kidding? He'd wanted to call the police since he'd first found out she had lied about Doug's call.

And she knew how much restraint it was taking on his part not to make that call.

They walked toward the house. Unlike the gaudy jumble of Christmas lights in Derek Ernst's neighborhood, or the friendly cheer in Detective Baker's, this house was decorated like something out of a magazine. Perfect wreaths adorned each door and several windows, and a gentle sprinkle of white lights lent a magical mood. Very lush, very tasteful, yet a little too slick to feel either warm or joyous.

Salt ground under their feet on the plowed concrete drive. The night had grown colder, and the air prickled the inside of her nose with each inhaled breath. "Do you think Connor might be in there?"

"I don't know. Maybe. I do think that if he's not, there's a very good chance Ms. Vickery knows where he is."

That was what she was hoping for. That was what she was hanging on to.

They followed the sidewalk, mounting the curved steps that led to the bright red door. Ty rang the bell. Chimes echoed through the house.

Ten seconds passed, twenty, the time creeping slow as an ice floe. He pushed the button again. He leaned toward one of the door's sidelights. Cupping his hand to shield the bright moon from reflecting on the glass, he peered inside. "Would you look at that?"

"What?" Megan brought her face close.

He pointed at something hanging on the wall of the foyer, close to the door.

Megan knew what the panel was immediately. "A

security system." And right there at the bottom of the screen was the name Keating Security. "But I don't remember the name Vickery from the client list."

"She's not the client."

"Who is?"

"Now that's a good damn question, isn't it? One we'll have to ask." He rang the bell again.

"She's not home." Megan hadn't realized how hopeful she was until she felt the sinking feeling inside.

"Or she doesn't want us to think she is, at any rate. Who knows? But one thing's for sure."

"What's that?" Megan could use something to count on. Something that was a sure thing.

"The woman who lives in this house is not walking the malls, trolling for a computer nerd boyfriend to steal. And even if she was, she wouldn't be desperate enough to go for Derek Ernst."

He was right about that. Megan couldn't imagine two people who seemed more incompatible.

Ty stepped off the walk and into the snow. He reached out a hand for Megan. "Let's have a look around."

Megan grasped his hand and followed. She was almost getting used to this sneaking around, trespassing stuff. More snow had filled her boots by the time they reached the back patio. Well, on most houses it might be called a patio. This one looked grand enough to be considered a snow-covered Disney World.

Tiered gardens and paths led in swirls down the steep bank. Every few feet, the path jutted off to a bench or a covered hot tub or some sort of garden feature Megan couldn't decipher under the blanket of snow. Trees dotted the gardens, spruce here and a naked clump of white-barked birch there and the occasional gnarled branches of oak. At the bottom of the steep slope, an inlet of Lake Hubbard stretched flat before them, smooth snow glowing blue in the moonlight. On the opposite bank stood an even larger mansion, rimmed with a wrought iron fence and twinkling with Christmas lights. "Harris House. This really is quite the neighborhood."

Ty nodded. "Most of the houses in this area were built during prohibition. They have secret rooms and tunnels used by the Chicago mob to hide their hooch."

Megan tried not to think of Connor trapped in one of those rooms. Scared. Hungry. She shook her head.

They circled the swimming pool drained for winter, only a few feet of water at the bottom. They stepped onto the cleared walkway and stomped the snow from their boots.

Ty cupped his hands as he had in the front of the house and peered inside. "These windows are wired. There's no way we can get in without setting off the alarm."

"Are all of these houses alarmed?"

"Most of them. As a patrol officer, I've never really kept up. I've just gone where the dispatcher sends me. We usually get at least half a dozen burglary calls from this neighborhood, during the off-season."

"These are vacation homes?"

"Most of them. Funny how the other half lives, eh?"

Megan sidled up to one of the many other windows and took a look.

The house was as opulent on the inside as it was on the outside. Marble floors stretched under plush oriental rugs. A dining room table inlaid with the iridescent shine of mother-of-pearl stretched in front of the window. The walls were filled with what looked like an antique buffet and matching china cabinets, but there were no dishes inside. No flowers on the table. Nothing but a thin sheet of dust.

She strained to see farther into the darkness. She could make out a staircase beyond, stretching up to who-knew-where. A hallway fading into shadows. No Christmas decorations on the inside. It was as if the house was an expensive but vacant shell. "It doesn't look like anyone actually lives here. Do you see anything?"

"No." He skipped a few windows and peered through the glass again. "Even the kitchen. No appliances on the countertops, nothing. If Samantha Vickery brought Derek here recently, they didn't seem to leave a lot of evidence behind."

"We've reached a dead end?" Not again. Not when she'd thought they were getting close to something. Close to finding her little boy.

She stepped back from the window, dizzy. *Connor. Where are you?*

"You okay?"

Megan turned, facing the pool. She blinked back tears and forced a nod, although it was a lie. "I thought we were on to something. I was hoping, but…"

He stepped up behind her. He pulled her back against his chest, and wrapped his arms around her waist. He kissed her temple. His breath felt warm on the side of her cheek.

She closed her eyes. Leaning against him, she soaked

in the solid feel of his chest, the strength of his arms holding her. Throughout all of this, one thing had been consistent. Whenever she lost hope, whenever she needed someone, Ty had been there. Holding her. Propping her up. Coming up with ideas of what they could do next.

She turned in his arms and tilted up her face to his. She wanted to feel him, know he was there. She wanted to soak in his strength, his passion, his love. And somehow, if she did, she hoped she might get through this.

He brought his mouth down on hers. His lips were hot, and they moved over hers with a hunger that stole her breath. There was no holding back this time, and she didn't hold back, either. She tangled her tongue with his, caressing, demanding. She wanted more than kisses from Ty. She wanted everything. Not just sex but love. Not just for now but forever. And for the first time in a long time, she felt bold enough to reach out and take.

Almost.

She pulled back from his lips and leaned her head on his chest.

He did nothing, said nothing. He just held her, as if he knew exactly what she needed, as if he'd provide it for her always, without needing to be asked.

Once they found Connor, she'd like to think this could continue. Grow past what they'd had as kids. Grow into something she could count on. A relationship like she'd always dreamed of. Passionate and exciting, sure. But what she longed for more than that giddy kind of love, what she'd wanted all her life, was someone she could meld with, grow comfortable with, grow old with.

Something she'd never had before. Something she didn't believe existed.

Until now.

She opened her eyes and blinked against the cold. The pool stretched before them, gaping like a hungry mouth. And from this angle, deep at the bottom, highlighted by moonlight, she could make out the form of a body under thick snow.

Chapter Fourteen

No matter how long Ty stared at the shape in the snow, it wasn't going to change what it was. And it wasn't going to melt away. "You know what this means?"

"We have to call the police?"

He gave a nod and reached for his cell phone. "We're going to have to come clean. You understand that, right, Meg? We're going to have to tell them everything."

He could feel her tremble under his arm.

"What will that mean? For Connor?"

"It will be okay." He angled Megan's body so she had to look him in the eye. "It will. They'll help. We should have let them help from the beginning."

Her eyelids dropped, moonlight casting shadows, making her eyelashes look impossibly long against her cheeks. "I'm so scared."

"I know. I'll be here with you the whole way." He pulled her close for just one more moment. He was afraid, too. More afraid than he wanted Megan to know. But it wasn't the police involvement that scared him. It was the kidnapper's call. He and Megan still knew so little, and if that was Samantha Vickery at the bottom of that pool, those who could have told them more were dead. The kidnapper seemed to be tying up loose ends. He just hoped and prayed Connor wasn't one of those ends. Megan either.

He had to protect them at all costs.

He gave her one last squeeze, then he pulled out his cell phone and made the call.

It didn't take long for the police to arrive. Of course, Ty's fellow patrol cops got there first. They cordoned off the area and put Ty and Megan into a black-and-white to warm up and wait for detectives.

Ty shifted on the hard plastic seat. He eyed the metal grate that separated the front seats from the rear compartment. He felt like a damn suspect. Worse, all he could think about was the many times he'd transported drunks in the back seat of his squad…and how many times they'd gotten sick.

He should have insisted they wait in his car.

Baker and a night shift sergeant named Jessica Taylor arrived next. Finally Leo showed up, his usually square haircut slightly askew, as if he'd been roused out of bed and hadn't thought to look in a mirror.

He opened the passenger door of the squad car and slipped inside, peering at them through the metal grate. "Hello there, Ty. You're a hard man to reach."

"Been busy."

"I see that." He turned his assessing eyes on Megan. "Hello, Ms. Garvey."

Ty didn't mind Leo's tone toward him. After the past day of ducking his calls, Ty certainly deserved what he got. But the skeptical way he was looking at Megan made

Ty want to throw his body between them to protect her. "We need to talk to you, Leo."

"I'll say." He settled fully into the seat, twisting around to give them both a good glare. "Why don't we start with you explaining how the two of you came to be spending this frigid night walking around peering into rich people's swimming pools?"

"The woman who lives in this house was at the mall the day Megan's son was kidnapped. She talked to me right at the moment the boy was taken."

"Hold on a second here." He zeroed in on Megan.

Ty shifted forward on the slick plastic seat. "Her name is Samantha Vickery. She was also involved with Derek Ernst, the mall guard who was manning the security cams that day. You know, the guy who supposedly shot himself up on Quarry Road."

Leo looked totally confused, but Ty pushed on without taking a breath, wanting to get all of it out there before the lieutenant had a chance to start grilling Megan. "It you want proof they knew each other, ask Ernst's old girlfriend and take a look at the nude photo of Vickery on Ernst's computer wallpaper. They were working together, Leo. They had to be. The two of them and the guy in the parka who grabbed Connor. They conspired to kidnap Megan's son."

Leo held up his hands, fingers splayed. "Hold on, Davis. What the hell are you talking about? There was no kidnapping." He searched Ty's face, then again focused on Megan. He didn't say a word, but the pressure in the car increased.

"I lied." Megan's voice sounded strong and clear, even

though her skin shone pale as the snow outside. "Doug didn't take Connor. Someone else did. My son has actually been kidnapped, and I have no idea where he is."

Ty leaned forward, balancing on the seat's slick edge. "The kidnapper demanded Megan stay away from police."

Even through the steel bars between the seats, Ty could see that Leo kept his eyes on Megan, as if he hadn't heard a word Ty said.

"He said if I didn't, I would never see my son again."

"He also demanded a ransom," Ty added. He tried to read Leo, but his square features revealed nothing.

Finally the lieutenant shook his head. "Let me get this straight. You lied about your ex-husband taking your son?"

"Yes."

"That's not possible."

Now it was Ty's turn to be confused. It might not have been wise, but it certainly was possible. Even understandable. "She was afraid for her son's life. The kidnapper was watching her apartment."

"I know it wasn't smart to lie. When Ty found out, he tried to talk me into telling you the truth. I wouldn't. I was afraid...afraid the kidnapper would hurt Connor. He said he would. Every time I talked to the police, he seemed to know."

"Hold on. Wait just a minute." Leo held up both hands. He focused on Ty. "You know we have to follow up in cases like these. You don't think I just took Doug Burke's word that he had his son and the boy was okay, do you?"

"Of course I wouldn't think that. I figured the snow storm and the Ernst shooting must have slowed you down."

He shook his head again, as if he had water in his ears he was trying to clear. "But I *have* followed up."

"Then you know this already."

Megan flew forward, her nose almost hitting the steel grate. "Are you out looking for Connor?"

"We don't have to look for Connor. We found him."

"What?" Her eyes grew saucer wide.

Leo's brows turned down and he looked at her as if she was a bit crazy. "He's with his father, just like you told me, Ms. Garvey."

"With his father?" Megan's head snapped around and she stared at Ty. "Doug really *does* have Connor?"

Ty didn't know what to think. Could Connor really have been with his father all along? "Is Doug playing some kind of joke on you?"

Megan shook her head. "I don't… It wasn't his voice on the phone. At least I don't think so."

Leo glanced back and forth between Megan and Ty. "You said there was a ransom demand. What did the kidnapper ask for?"

Megan teetered a little, looking as if she was about to fall over.

Ty grasped her hand. "He wanted the security information for clients of Keating Security."

"I work for Brilliance Cleaning," Megan explained. Her complexion was still ghostly, but she straightened her spine, as if willing the shock away. "Keating Security is one of the businesses I clean. And I have a background in computer work."

"So the alarm at Keating's last night?"

"I missed an extra layer of security in their system."

"Did you succeed in stealing the information?"

"No."

"Do you have any reason to believe your ex-husband would hurt your son?"

Megan shook her head. "No. No way."

"You said the voice on the phone wasn't Doug. Are you sure he wasn't just disguising his voice? Making you think it was someone else?"

"I...I don't know. But even if it is Doug, he's pretending he's a kidnapper. He's asking for ransom. Isn't that a crime?"

"I have to be honest, Ms. Garvey, we will look into this, but there might not be a lot we can do. Your husband has his own son, and you gave him permission. He didn't lie to the police. You did."

Ty opened his mouth.

Leo held up a hand. "But if we can come up with some evidence of threats, of blackmail, maybe we can do something. But he could argue that you just changed your mind about him visiting with his son. Really, this is something that's best to resolve between you and your ex-husband. Getting police involved in stuff like this can turn into a big mess where nobody wins. And there's the Keating problem. That can't just go away, whether you were successful or not."

The lieutenant was right. She'd fallen smack into

whatever scheme Doug had planned. "Are you saying you can't do anything?"

He offered her an apologetic look. "One thing that might help is documentation of the calls. Do you have a record of the incoming phone number?"

Megan rummaged in her bag until she located her cell. She flipped it open and brought up the number for the last incoming call and handed the phone to the lieutenant. "He told me the number was not traceable back to him."

"That doesn't mean he was telling the truth. I don't know if this will get us anything at all, but I can talk to him, see what he has to say for himself." He glanced at Ty. "And of course, we'll look into this Vickery woman. But from what we have now, I don't see a conspiracy to commit anything."

Ty slid back in the seat. Could Leo be right? "How could all of these connections be coincidences? I don't buy it."

"Maybe they aren't coincidences. But we're going to have to let the investigation determine that. If this Vickery woman is the body in the pool, we'll turn her life upside down. If this is her house, you can be sure we'll look into her pretty carefully. Believe me, if there's something else there, we'll find it. But whatever happens, except for writing some statements for me about how you came to discover this body in someone's backyard, your role in this is over."

"Over," Megan whispered. She tilted her eyes to the ceiling, scooped in a deep breath, then leveled her gaze back on Leo. "You said you saw him? Connor?"

"Yesterday. I stopped at the hotel on the way home."

Ty couldn't keep himself from lurching forward again. "They're here? In Lake Hubbard?"

"The motor lodge up by the interstate. The one with the pool."

"How was Connor?" Megan's voice trembled. "Was he okay?"

Leo's face finally softened. "Seemed like a happy little kid having fun with his dad. I really didn't think there was anything else to it. Figured Doug must have been jealous of Davis here, playing Santa Claus. Didn't want another man winning over his son."

Megan nodded and slumped a little against the seat.

"I'll send Baker to get your statements and then you can go." He opened the door.

A wave of cold air rushed over them.

He climbed out of the squad car, then leaned back into the open door. "And Ty? We're extending your suspension a couple more days, but neither the chief nor I want you to think it reflects on you. I'd just rather keep you away from the media. They seem to be looking to blow this 'Wannabe Santa' thing into their latest feel-good scandal of the holiday season. Next time, go through the department for real, and don't be paying for Shop with a Cop out of your own pocket."

Ty barely heard the car door slam. He was too busy focusing on Megan's shocked stare.

Chapter Fifteen

Megan's head spun. The past few minutes had flipped her life around completely. First finding a dead body. Then learning Doug had Connor this whole time. And now…"What did he say?"

"I was going to tell you."

"Tell me what?"

Ty looked miserable, and sheepish, and guilty as hell. "I just thought you and Connor deserved a nice Christmas."

"Connor and I…you told me that the police department had extra money. That they didn't have enough kids in the program this year to use all the donations, but… but it was all you? The money came from you?"

"I wanted to do something for you. I knew you wouldn't accept it if you knew it was from me."

"Damn right, I wouldn't have accepted it. You lied to me."

"I'm sorry."

"You kept this from me this whole time."

"I'm sorry."

"I feel like such an idiot." She held up her hand. "If you say you're sorry again, I'm going to punch you."

He pressed his lips into a hard line. "I don't know what to say then. What is it you want to hear?"

Her throat felt thick. The truth was, she didn't know. Here she'd convinced herself she could trust Ty, that she could rely on him, accept his help. That it was *okay* to accept his help. But this wasn't okay. "It's like those gifts my father gave my mother."

He frowned and shook his head, not following.

"He bought her gifts. Jewelry mostly. Every time he came back from what he was calling a business trip, he brought her something nice. A necklace. A pair of earrings. A bracelet. And the whole time, he wasn't away on business at all. He was staying with his girlfriend."

"Now wait just a second—"

"I know you're not him. You haven't done anything to hurt me. Ever. I know that up here." She tapped her forehead. "But it feels the same." She pressed her hand to her chest. Her heart slammed against her ribs, so hard it felt like it would smash through.

She knew it was impossible to make Ty understand. She didn't really understand herself. But she had to try. "The whole Shop with a Cop thing, it was…a manipulation. And I can't live through that. Not again. Even if you were just trying to do something nice."

"I know you don't want to hear me say I'm sorry again, but I am. I wasn't trying to…" He looked down. "God, Meg, I didn't really believe there was anything left between us, not when I called you about Shop with a Cop. I mean, I hoped for it. And I wanted an excuse to see you again. But I wasn't trying to trick you into anything."

She let out a heavy breath and tangled her fingers in her lap. She wanted to believe him. She did believe him, but that didn't change how betrayed she felt. How confused. She wanted, just once, to not have to worry about ulterior motives and nice gestures being manipulations in disguise. Just once she wanted things to be exactly as they seemed.

"I didn't mean for this to get so blown out of proportion. I really just wanted to make things better for you and Connor. I know it was a stupid way to do that. And God knows, it didn't work out very well. But it's what I wanted. It's what you deserve."

She shook her head. "You keep saying that. That I deserve better. What I deserve, Ty, is the truth. I deserve to be able to trust that you'll give it to me, no matter what."

She opened the door and climbed out into the cold. She couldn't look at him a moment longer. Couldn't listen to him say he was sorry one more time. She wanted to believe everything he said, to let it go, to fall into his arms and just pretend it all didn't exist. But that was what her mother had done. She'd run away from the truth until she couldn't run anymore. Until the only alternative was to try to poison herself with sleeping pills so she didn't have to face her husband's double life.

She'd almost succeeded. And now she would likely live the rest of her days in a nursing home. Five years, and she still hadn't recovered from the lack of oxygen to her brain.

Megan turned into the wind starting to kick up over the lake. The chill slapped her face, tears freezing on her cheeks. She heard the squad door open behind her and started walking. She didn't want him to catch up with her. She didn't want to hear any more. "Please. I just need to be alone."

"Megan."

"No. I mean it. Give me some time. Please."

"Fine. Okay," he yelled into the wind. "I'll go see what's happening at the pool."

She gave him a nod, anything, just so he'd go.

"I'll come back in a few minutes, and check how you're feeling. Okay?"

Feeling? What should she be feeling? Furious? Shaken? She didn't know. Her insides were such a jumble of different emotions, all she felt was numb. But she did know that if Ty talked to her, listened to her, put his arm around her and pulled her close, that she wouldn't be able to see anything straight. And she couldn't let that happen. Before she was near him again, she needed to think. "Okay, fine."

His footsteps crunched on snow, moving away.

She let out a breath.

Mind still reeling, she walked to a rise between one mansion and the next. From here she could see the top of the garden labyrinth overlooking the lake. Police spotlights glowed from behind the mansion. The wind felt good against her cheeks, like a cold slap of reality. She let it buffet her, turning her fresh tears to ice.

The bleat of her cell phone shattered the cold night.

A hum of panic rose in Megan's ears, overcoming the

sound of the wind. She glanced back, looking for Ty, but he was already circling the house, heading for the glowing lights and the body at the bottom of the partially drained pool. She was on her own.

She reached into her bag and pulled out the phone. She took a deep breath of frigid air, pushed the answer button and held it to her ear. "Hello?"

"You have the files?"

The voice shivered through her. It might sound a little like Doug. But even now, she wouldn't have pegged it. Whatever he was doing to alter his voice, it had worked on her.

She glanced back toward the house and the aurora of police lights glowing behind it. Lieutenant Wheeling was right. This was between her and her ex-husband. "Where's Connor?"

"You bring the files, you can have the boy."

The boy. Sounding tough. Sounding like Connor wasn't his very own son. The bastard. "Where?"

"Chicago. At the aquarium. Tomorrow."

She set her chin. She was tired of being manipulated. By Doug. By Ty. All of them. She'd had enough. She wanted Connor back now. It was time to take control. "Not tomorrow. Now."

"What?"

"I want Connor back now. Bring him to my apartment, and I'll give you the files."

"It doesn't work that way."

"From now on, it does. I know this is you, Doug. And I know you have Connor. You showed him to a police lieutenant last night." Her head spun. She couldn't believe so much had happened in less than two days. So much worry. So much fear. So much of what she'd even wanted to think could be love. It was hard to sort through it all.

At least she knew how to handle Doug. She had no illusions about him. She wondered if she ever had. "I'm done with this, Doug. No more threats. No more manipulation. If you want these damn security files, you'd better give Connor to me now. Otherwise, I'll just hand them over to the police."

"You do that. Remember, you're the one who has committed the crime here. I'll bring Connor to prison to visit you."

Right. She'd been the one to break into Keating's computers. And if she actually had gotten the files, she wouldn't want anyone to know what she'd done. Even now, there might be repercussions when this shook out. After all the capers she and Ty had been involved in over the last hours, she still couldn't think like a criminal. "Fine. I'll throw it in the lake. Happy?"

"Barisi Park, the Lake Street entrance. Be there in ten minutes. Alone."

She made the time calculation in her mind. She didn't have her car. If she asked to borrow Ty's, he would insist on coming along. She really wasn't sure she could handle that right now. She wasn't sure where to turn. "I can't get there that quickly."

"If you think I'm going to delay this so you have time to get the police involved, you're out of your mind. You said now. I'll give you now."

"Give me twenty."

"Twenty, then. And come alone," he repeated, as if she might have forgotten that part. "Totally alone."

"Or what, Doug? What are you going to do to me? You and I both know you aren't going to hurt Connor." Even though she felt like spitting on him for pretending to threaten their son, she had to admit she was relieved that Connor had never been in any danger. "Things have changed, Doug. You've lost your power over me."

"Keating Security and the police will both get phone calls, and I'll buy the boy a new suit to wear to your trial. How about that?"

"Whatever." She clapped the phone shut. Doug held no sway over her anymore, not that he had in a long while. Not when she'd known she was dealing with him.

And while she still felt alone and confused walking away from Ty and back toward town, she felt stronger and more fearless than she had in what seemed like a long time.

And maybe that was a trade-off she would have to accept.

TY CIRCLED THE EDGE OF THE house, watching Megan's silhouette against the moon's glow on the lake. The last thing he'd wanted to do was leave her alone. But what could he do? He certainly couldn't help this time. He'd never felt more useless in his life.

He'd been stupid lying about the Shop with a Cop money. He'd been even more stupid not to tell Megan about it yesterday. But he knew she'd push him away if he had. And the thought of her dealing with Connor's kidnapping alone…he really couldn't live with that.

Of course, the kidnapping had all been a lie, too.

So what happened now?

He had no answers. No idea what to do next. All he knew was that any feelings between them that had been revived were gone. Not on his part. Never on his part. But on hers. He doubted she'd be able to trust him after this.

He rounded the corner of the house. Spotlights glared off snow, turning the paths, tiered gardens and pool area brighter than day. He blinked and willed his eyes to adjust.

Lake Hubbard didn't have a big police department, but it seemed as though almost everyone on the night shift was here. Sergeant Taylor stood at the edge of the drained pool. Baker held a camera, and a detective by the name of Johnson was documenting everything on video. Ty had noticed the deputy coroner arrive while he was talking to Megan, but he didn't see the man milling at the scene. Leo stood away from the pool, a cell phone clapped to his ear.

"What's up, Davis?" His old pal Ed Sheffield walked up the path toward him. With his overcoat hunched around his shoulders and billowing out from his sides, his silhouette looked as if he was wearing some kind of cape. The glare of the lights sparkled in the gray threading his hair, and his mustache was covered with frost.

"Have they shoveled out the body?" Ty craned his neck to see. Impossible from this angle.

"Don't know. The coroner just went down into the pool."

Ty stepped forward, and Ed angled his body slightly to block his path.

Ty nodded toward the pool. "Oh, come on, Ed. You don't really mind if I take a look?"

"You know how it works, Ty."

"I found the damn body. My footprints are already all over the place."

"And that's a reason I should let you trample the scene a little more?"

"I won't trample anything. The body was under a load of snow. There aren't going to be any tracks that mean anything. Besides, I'm a cop, remember?"

"Then you should understand."

Ty glanced to the other side of the house. Trevor stood near the far corner, staring out at the lake. Just his luck to have approached from Ed's side. He could probably get past the younger cop.

His breath billowed in front of him and then whipped away in the wind curling and swirling around the corner of the house. Damn, it was cold. "You really going to make me stand here and wait until Leo or Jess decide to amble this way?"

"Life's a bitch sometimes."

"You're a cruel man."

Ed nodded, as if he was a bit proud of that fact.

Ty let out a dramatic sigh. "I guess I should aim to be more like you, shouldn't I?"

Ed gave him a suspicious look.

"And with that in mind, on my very next shift, I'll rededicate myself to stopping speeders on Massing Road. One mile an hour over, and they get a ticket. Wait, that's in your neighborhood, isn't it, Ed?" Ty let his words sink in. Ed's teenage son had a talent for collecting speeding tickets even though most patrol cops in Lake Hubbard tried to take it easy on the kid. It was an unfair threat, maybe even cruel, like Ty promised. But he would bet the thought of driving the kid around after his license was revoked wouldn't make Ed's night.

Ed rubbed his mustache. "If anyone asks, it was Trevor who let you through."

Ty grinned. "Thanks, man. And tell your kid to slow down anyway."

Ed nodded. "I'll tell him you're a manipulative SOB."

Ty tried to laugh, but it wouldn't come. Megan would probably agree with that statement about now.

Ty slipped past Ed and traced the path he and Megan had walked when they'd first arrived, when they'd been looking for a live woman, not a dead one. He could still feel Megan's very live body snugged into his, leaning against him. It was simple, he knew, but the way he felt whenever she let him hold her or when she leaned on him…as if he was strong enough to take on anything.

There was no better feeling in the world.

It seemed so long ago since he'd experienced that high, even though only barely over an hour had passed since they'd found the body.

An hour which had changed everything.

He pulled a frigid breath into his lungs. At least they knew Connor was with Doug. That he had never been in danger. That alone was enough for him to hold on to.

The rest…he would just have to hope Megan would see reason once she realized he hadn't meant any harm.

But he wouldn't bet on it.

Leo looked up as he approached. The bright lights glared down on him. The wind had really picked up on this side of the house and its chill showed in Leo's face, his cheeks a dark shade of pink that looked like sunburn. "Davis? What are you doing here?"

"How is everything going?" He tried to make his voice sound casual, but he wasn't sure he'd succeeded.

"Not well." Leo exchanged looks with Sergeant Jessica Taylor.

She stepped out, as if to bar Ty's way. "Where is Megan Garvey?"

"She's back by the cars."

"You need to go back by the cars, too." She glanced back toward the pool.

"So let me get a look at what's going on, and I will." They'd found something. Something Leo and Jess were nervous about letting him see. "I'm going to find out sooner or later."

The sergeant glanced back at Leo.

He nodded his blond head. "He's right. Might as well let him see for himself."

Sergeant Taylor moved to the side, making room for him to step to the pool's edge.

For a moment, he couldn't see anything, the lights were so bright. As his eyes adjusted, he focused on the body deep in the pool, lying at the deputy coroner's feet.

He expected to see blond hair. Too much eyeliner. The

face of the woman who'd called herself the Giftinator. But it wasn't Samantha Vickery. It wasn't a woman at all. The body at the bottom of the pool was a man. And his face...

The ground tilted and started to spin under Ty's feet as he looked into the frozen eyes of Doug Burke.

Chapter Sixteen

Ty blinked. The bright light must be playing tricks on him. Yet he knew what he was seeing was real. Doug. Dead.

And if Megan's ex-husband was here, where was Connor?

Ty looked over at Leo. "You said you talked to Doug last night. That you saw him."

"I did. And yes, he was very much alive then."

Ty sifted the facts through his mind. The body was totally covered with snow when he and Megan discovered it. That meant Doug had to be dead before the brunt of the storm hit Lake Hubbard. That didn't give Leo much time to check up on him before he was killed. "When exactly did you see him?"

Leo waved the question away. "We don't have time to discuss this, Ty. Where is Megan Garvey?"

An uneasy feeling pinched the back of Ty's neck. "She's back by the cars."

Leo shook his head. "I just talked to Trevor. She's not there."

"Not there? Impossible. Where would she have gone?"

"You tell me. We need to talk to her. Now."

He didn't know. But he was damn well going to find her. But not so Leo could interrogate her. Doug being dead changed everything. It meant Connor was still out there. Still in danger. It meant they had to figure out what they were going to do about that and fast, before the kidnapper called. "Leave finding Megan to me. What are you going to do about Connor?"

Leo looked stunned, as if he hadn't yet put together the fact that if Doug was here, he couldn't have Connor any longer. He glanced at Sergeant Taylor. "We need to begin a search."

"Where do we start?"

"The hotel. Here. Call the county, ask them to bring in dogs. It's damn cold out here for a kid. Go, go, go."

Sergeant Taylor raced up the path toward Ed, already barking orders.

"Ty?" Leo said.

Ty stopped midstride and turned around.

"I don't know what's going on here, but we need to get to the bottom of it." He glanced from Ty to the body then back again, as if not sure where to focus, his normally intense glare scattered.

It was the first time Ty had ever seen Leo look shaken.

Ty raced back around the house, past Taylor, Ed and Trevor, getting into their cars. He scanned the area where he'd last seen Megan. Nothing but cold and snow and wind.

Where the hell did she go?

The call. Maybe the kidnapper had already called. But if he had, wouldn't she have told him about it? Even if she still thought the kidnapper was Doug, wouldn't she at least ask for a ride back to his house to pick up her car? Or had he damaged her trust so badly, she wouldn't accept his help even in this?

It didn't matter. None of it did. Whether she wanted his help or not, she would get it. And if she hated him for it in the end, then that was just the way it was.

But first, he had to find her.

He opened his car door and had the engine started almost the moment he slid behind the wheel. He shifted into gear and hit the accelerator. The car skidding on ice and snow, he powered out of the driveway and onto the road.

Where would she go? To his house? Downtown? Downtown was closer, just on the other side of the inlet. But how far could she get without a car?

He reached a branch in the road and took the street that led around the finger of lake and toward downtown. He'd just rounded a curve when he spotted her red hair in his headlight beam.

He'd found her. Thank God. He swung to the curb alongside her and exhaled a breath. Now he just had to figure out how to break the news.

MEGAN HEARD THE SOUND OF A CAR pulling to the curb, and without even looking, she knew it was Ty.

"Megan," he called.

She spared him a glance but kept walking. She still

had blocks to go, and time was ticking away too quickly. She couldn't afford to slow down. "What is it?"

Driver's door open, he propped himself half out of his seat and shouted to her over the windshield. "You've got to get in the car."

"I can't."

"Listen to me, Megan. Everything has changed. Leo needs to talk to you. We need to figure out what to do next."

"I know what I'm doing next. I'm going to get my son. As soon as he's safe in my arms, I'll listen to whatever you and anyone else has to say."

"You're going to get Connor?"

She hadn't wanted to tell him. She knew he was going to insist on coming with her. The closer she got to Barisi Park, the less strong and more unsure she felt. But even so, she wasn't certain having Ty around would do anything more than add confusion to the list. "This is between me and Doug. I'm handling it alone."

"Doug?"

She didn't know if Ty was just trying to be difficult, or if the wind had grown so loud he was having trouble hearing. But either way, she didn't have time for this. "He called. I'm meeting him. I'm getting Connor back. I don't need you, Ty."

"Megan, get in."

She shook her head and kept walking. "I'm handling this. I don't need your help. I don't want it."

"Doug is dead, Meg."

She couldn't have heard him right. She stopped and stared at the car. "What?"

"The body in the pool. It wasn't Samantha Vickery. It was Doug."

Her mind stuttered. Doug? Dead? How was that possible? "I just talked to him. He has Connor. What are you saying?"

"He's dead, Meg."

Her vision spun. She was going to be sick. She was going to lose her balance and topple headlong into the snow. "The lieutenant said…"

"Doug must have been killed after he talked to Leo."

She shook her head. "The body we found was totally covered with snow. How is that possible?"

"I don't know." Judging from the lines in his forehead, he was troubled by the timing and coincidence of it all as much as she was. "You said you talked to Doug?"

"He called. Only it wasn't Doug, was it? It was a real kidnapper. And I told him…" The memory of how forceful and demanding she'd been lurched through her mind. She'd demanded he meet her now, here in Lake Hubbard. She insisted on ten minutes more so she'd have time to walk to the park. All that, and here she didn't even have the files he wanted.

"What did you tell him?"

She filled him in on her brazen responses.

A smile of surprise and even admiration curled the corners of Ty's lips. "When are you supposed to meet him?"

Time. They were running out of time. She looked at her watch. "Oh my God. I have to be there in five minutes."

"Get in the car."

She shook her head. "He said to come alone."

"Get in the car. I'll drive you part of the way. It's the only way you're going to make it."

She reached for the door handle before she could re-think her decision. Now that she knew she wasn't dealing with Doug, she hadn't a clue what to do next. She yanked the door open and jumped into the seat. Strapping her seat belt on, she slammed the door and twisted to face him. "I'm supposed to meet him at the Lake Street en-trance of Barisi Park."

Ty pulled away from the curb.

"He said to come alone."

"You're not going to be able to do that. He's killed two people we know of. Maybe Samantha Vickery, too. And you don't have the files. He's not going to let you or Connor walk out of that park."

As he said the words, she knew they were true. "So what do I do? He has my baby." She choked back a sob. She didn't have time for emotion now. She had to think. They had to figure out a way to get Connor back unhurt.

"You have the flash drive?"

She patted the small bulge in her pocket, even though she knew it was there. "Yes."

"You're going to have to pretend it holds the files. Can you do that?"

"Yes." She could. She had to. "What if he checks?"

"We hope I can get you and Connor out of there before he does."

"Seems like a long shot. Seems like he won't let me have Connor until he checks. I wouldn't if I were him."

"That's why I'm calling for help."

A tremor seized her stomach. "The police?"

"It's the only way, Megan. It would be better if we had time to get into place, call for the county SWAT team. But this will have to do. At least they'll be armed. We can even our odds a bit."

"What if Connor gets shot?"

"Like you said, he'll probably check the flash drive before he gives you Connor, that is, if he intends to give you Connor at all."

"You don't think he'll have Connor in the park?"

"I wouldn't." He pressed his lips into a line.

"So how do we find out where he is?"

"I don't know. We'll figure something out. Play along with him as long as you can. And if he wants you to do anything or turn over the flash drive, insist on seeing Connor first."

He swung to the curb and stopped the car. "I'd better let you out here. You can walk the rest of the way."

"And you?"

"I'll call it in. And I'll be with you in the park."

"But he said—"

"He won't see me." He grasped her arm, pulled her close and kissed her. The kiss wasn't tender or sexy, but desperate. A promise. "I love you, Megan. I won't let anything happen to you or to Connor. We'll get him back. Just act as if you're totally alone, just the way he wanted. I'll do the rest."

She nodded and brought her fingers to her lips, trying

to catch her breath, trying to grasp the jumble of emotions turning her inside out.

She'd play along. She'd let Ty take care of the rest. There was no one she trusted as much.

Chapter Seventeen

Even though she was fully clothed and wrapped to the gills in a black wool coat and thick scarf, Samantha Vickery looked just like the picture on Derek Ernst's computer. Megan marched up to the woman who had been in on Connor's kidnapping from the beginning. The only thing keeping her from punching the blonde in the face was the pistol clutched in her black-gloved hand.

She smiled and pushed her hair back over one shoulder with her non-gun-holding hand. "You've brought the security files?"

Megan nodded, not trusting her voice to function.

"Then walk. That way." She gestured down the sidewalk with her gun.

Megan glanced into the park. Moonlight glowed off the kids' sledding hill. Snow lay thick on the play structure, making it look more like an igloo than slides and bridges. Swings moved in the wind, the creak of the chains eerie in the cold night. She didn't know if Ty was in there or not. But she hoped that wherever he was, he noticed them moving. And she hoped the woman was taking her to Connor.

They walked along a row of arborvitae, blocking the view of the park. More than once, Megan thought she heard the rustle of movement on the other side of the narrow yet dense evergreens. The crunch of a footstep in snow. The whisper of breath over the wind. Christmas lights sparkled from the storefronts ahead and along the back fence of Harris House. They crossed the street, leaving the park behind, and circled into the alley behind the shops.

There were no evergreens to hide behind here. No place to watch unseen, not unless Ty scaled the wrough iron fence. And still she didn't see a single sign of him. Had she walked to meet the Vickery woman too quickly? Had she failed to give Ty enough time to park his car, call the police and get into place? Had they left him behind?

The woman's footsteps slowed. "Stop. In here." A hand closed around Megan's arm and shoved her past a Dumpster and toward the back door of one of the shops.

Megan stumbled up the steps. Bracing her hands on the door, she looked up at the writing below the peephole expecting to see the Radiant Diamonds logo. At first her mind wouldn't absorb the word that was there.

Julianne's.

"You have the code. Get us in the door."

This had to be some kind of mistake. Samantha Vickery must have gotten her signals crossed.

"You heard me."

"You want me to break into a sex shop?"

"You know the codes, right? He said you would know the codes."

"*He* said? Who?"

"Just do it."

Megan scrambled for an answer. "I don't have the codes memorized. They're on a flash drive. I need a computer to read them."

"There's a computer inside. Open the door."

"I can't."

"Then your son dies. How about that?"

Judging from the hard look on the woman's face, she would be willing to carry out her threat herself.

Megan tamped down the panic bubbling deep inside. She stared at the door. There had to be some way to get in, didn't there? It was an old building. And if she remembered correctly, the system Keating had installed was very simple. She had to think. She had to figure out a way.

"Don't even think about setting off the alarm. If that happens, your son dies. It's all arranged. I don't even have to lift a finger. Hear me?"

Megan forced a nod. Her lungs contracted, too tight to breathe. She eyed the single window on one side of the door, too high for her to even touch the frame. A bank of windows flanked the other side, lower, within a tiptoe's reach of the step. If they weren't painted shut...

"Hurry up."

"If I hurry too much, I'll set the damn alarm off."

"That's your problem. Now do it."

She checked once again to make sure the windows weren't alarmed. Then she placed the heel of her hand right below the window lock, as Ty had done on Derek Ernst's garage. Doing her best to breathe, she gave the upper sash a hard rap.

Pain shot through her hand and down her arm. The window lock stayed in place.

"That's your plan?"

"You said to get us in without setting off the alarm. Be quiet and let me do it." She positioned her hand again and gave another upward blow.

The lock popped free.

A breath shuddered from her lungs. She slid the bottom sash upward. Now to climb inside. She positioned her foot on the rail and hoisted herself through the small space.

She pushed through heavy velvet curtains and landed on a shelving unit on the other side of the window. Various toys and gadgets clattered and bounced to the floor. She pulled herself through the rest of the way and turned back to the window.

Samantha Vickery glared at her from outside, the gun's barrel leveled on her chest. "If I don't show up, your son—"

"Is dead. I know. Now are you going to climb inside, or are you waiting for a cop car to drive by and see you?" Not that it was likely to happen that way in the isolated alley. She just had to pray Ty had his eye on them.

"Stand back from the window. Not so far that I can't see you."

Megan stepped back, and Samantha clambered inside.

Megan glanced around the dark shop. The mannequin

loomed near the front door, looking like a person watching. Chains and whips caught the light of a passing car's headlights.

Samantha cleared the frame just as the lights flitted across the front windows. She straightened and thrust the gun out in front of her once again. "To the office. Now."

Megan shuffled toward the door the camomile tea woman had emerged from, hoping that was the office Samantha was referring to. Even though the door was only a few feet away, the space was an obstacle course of cluttered shelves and dramatic displays. "Why are we here?"

"Just move. You weren't supposed to be part of this. But things have changed. Certain people have gotten cold feet and screwed everything up."

"You're talking about Doug?" Had Samantha Vickery killed him? He was in her pool. At least in the house where Corrine had seen her take Derek. "Or are you referring to Derek Ernst?"

"It's not my fault if they can't do what it takes."

"And what does it take? Being willing to kill an innocent child?"

"Listen, that isn't my idea, either. The kid was never supposed to be in any danger. Everything would be fine if that husband of yours wouldn't have gotten spooked by the cop."

The lieutenant. Was that how the timing worked? His visit had frightened Doug. And when Doug wanted out, they'd killed him?

Reaching the door, she glanced back at the blonde.

"What is all this about? It's certainly not about stealing sex toys and leather lingerie."

Samantha didn't answer, not that Megan expected her to. "Open the door."

Megan tried the knob. "It's locked."

"So open it."

Ty had shown her the trick with the window. She had no idea how to break in a locked door. "What do you think I am, an experienced burglar?"

"So look for a key. Try the top of the door frame."

She stretched to her tiptoes and felt the top of the frame. Her fingertips hit a piece of metal. She grasped it and took a look, straining to see in the darkness.

Sure enough, it was a thick metal wire twisted into the shape of a key. High-tech security, this was not.

She unlocked the door, and pushed it open.

Where the rest of Julianne's House of Pleasure looked like the old building that housed it, this room *was* truly high-tech. Two computers and various other equipment stretched along one side of the wall, stuff that was far more advanced than anything Megan had worked on, stuff that made even Derek Ernst's setup look rinky-dink. One computer was connected to a modem. One was not. "So that's why you seduced Derek. To get hold of his computer skills."

"You don't think I had the hots for him or something?"

"So why did you kill him?"

"I didn't."

The kidnapper. The male voice she'd heard on the phone. "Who did?"

"If I told you that, then destroying what we are about to destroy wouldn't really do much."

"What are we about to destroy?"

She hit the back of the computer chair, swiveling it around. "Sit."

Megan perched on the edge. "Now what?"

"Now you get into the computer."

"It's probably tied into the alarm system."

"That's why you're here. You and the codes you stole from the security company. You don't think I needed you just to get past the door alarm, do you?"

Megan stared at the monitor. She was shaking all over now, from her fingers to her feet. Not only did she not have the security information, but she'd proved to be not very good at defeating the computer security systems Keating had in place on its own computers. This was way over her head.

How in the world was she going to pull this off?

She opened the desk drawer, looking for any sign of a password. Except for a few pens, the drawer was empty.

"Well?"

Maybe if she could stall for time, Ty would be able to come up with something, wherever he was. She sure hoped he could, because she was running out of other options. "When I get into the system, what am I looking for?"

"First get in. I'll tell you what to do from there."

Megan tried to quell the tremble in her chest. She couldn't beat the computer's security system. Not without a password. Not without the Keating files.

"Well? What are you waiting for?"

Her bluff had been called. The ruse was over. There was only one thing left for her to do. What Ty had told her. "I'm not going to do this. Not until I see Connor. Not until I know he's unhurt."

"You're not going to see anybody if you don't get this done." Samantha raised the gun, as if she thought Megan needed a reminder that she was carrying a weapon.

Megan stared at the monitor. Ty said he'd be with her. He promised he'd have her back. He would keep his word. She knew it. He'd keep his word or he would die trying.

She leaned back in the chair, gripped the arms and held on. "I don't care. If my little boy isn't okay, I don't care about any of it."

"Oh, for crying out loud. Would everyone around here rather die than cooperate? This is unbelievable." Samantha Vickery reached for her cell with her free hand. She scrolled through her address book, hit a number and held the phone to her ear.

Megan held her breath.

"I know, I know. I didn't have a choice." Samantha Vickery shot her a poisonous glare. "She won't do it. Not until she sees the kid."

Little did the woman know, but Megan couldn't do what she wanted even then. She just had to trust Ty would get her and Connor out of this mess before the Giftinator and whoever she was talking to figured that out.

TY JOGGED DOWN THE SIDEWALK, his pistol clutched in one hand, his eyes riveted to Julianne's House of Pleasure ahead. His throat and head ached from the cold air, but he didn't dare slow his pace. It had taken longer than he'd thought to convince Ed and Trevor to help without reporting to Jess Taylor or Leo first. Ty wasn't worried about Sergeant Taylor, but he knew she'd tell Leo, and with the timing of Doug's death niggling at the back of Ty's mind, he'd rather not take the chance that Leo wasn't on the up and up.

Nearing the sex shop, he slowed to a walk and turned down the side street. The alley behind backed up to the wrought iron fence surrounding the vast Harris House grounds.

He slipped behind a Dumpster and focused on a single rear window to the right of the door. A light glowed through the slats of miniblinds. A shadow moved across the window. That had to be them inside, although what they were doing, he hadn't a clue.

He hunkered down beside the Dumpster to wait. Between the fence and the dead end alley, there was nowhere to go but past him.

If Megan had followed the plan, they would either have to bring the boy to her or her to the boy. At that point, it would be up to him. He just prayed Ed and Trevor were there to back him up.

"What are you doing here, Officer Davis?"

Ty whipped around, searching the darkness, trying to locate the speaker. A crack exploded in his ears and a bullet plowed into his chest.

Chapter Eighteen

Megan gasped at the pop of gunfire coming from outside the shop. Her mind raced. The kidnapper? *Ty? Connor?*

Samantha Vickery bolted to the window and peered between the blinds. "The computer. Now."

Megan shot to her feet, trying to see outside, as well.

The alley was dark, but she spotted the silhouette of a man. He was standing over something...no, *someone* on the ground.

"I said, get into that computer." Samantha shoved her back into the chair. She swung the gun barrel hard against Megan's cheek.

Megan's head whipped to the side. Pain shuddered through her skull and rang in her ears.

"If you want to see your son—"

"I can't."

"What do you mean, you can't? You have the codes."

What should she say? She couldn't do what the woman wanted. If she admitted she didn't have the codes, what then? Would Samantha kill her? Would she and whoever was out in the alley kill Connor?

Had they already?

A sob stuck in her throat. She couldn't breathe. She couldn't think.

"You do have the codes, don't you?" Samantha turned away from the window and faced Megan. She brought the gun up and pointed the barrel straight at her face.

Megan forced her voice to function. "The police will be here. Someone will call about the shot."

"Then you'd better make it quick."

She tried to clear her mind, to push the pain back, the panic.

Ty had wondered if Julianne's provided more than sex toys. He'd wondered if it was a front for prostitution. If she followed that line of thinking, she could guess what might be on the computers. Something scandalous. Something that could be used for blackmail. "If you want to destroy the computer's memory, we don't need the codes. We just take the computer and run. Dump it in the lake or something." At least then, they'd be out in the open. At least then Ty or another officer might be able to help.

The woman narrowed her heavily lined eyes to slits. "You never got the information from the security company?"

Although the truth was obvious at this point, Megan still didn't dare admit anything. "Just destroy the computer itself."

"Damn, damn, damn. I don't want to destroy everything on it. I didn't do all this just to save his ass."

Of course. Why hadn't Megan thought of it before? Samantha had said things didn't go as planned. And her words hinted that she didn't fully trust her partner in crime. Maybe Megan could use the woman's fear and mistrust to manipulate her, to catch her off guard. "He killed Derek Ernst, didn't he?"

The woman gave her a suspicious look.

"You certainly didn't plan for me to copy and destroy files at gunpoint."

Her lips flattened into a line, conceding the point.

"So what happened? Was Derek going to go to the police? Or did your partner just tell you that?"

"What are you saying?"

Megan shrugged, letting Samantha's own imagination fill in the blanks. "And Doug. I'm guessing dealing with a three-year-old child, maybe having to kill him, that wasn't your idea either, was it?"

The woman's eyes shifted to the window and then back to Megan.

"Was it?" Megan prodded.

"No."

"So who's next? Me, certainly. Maybe my son, too. Then what? Then who is a liability?" She gestured to the computer. "Because I can't get you into this thing. All I can do is help you destroy it."

The woman tightened her grip on the gun, her hands shaking. "He told me it would work out."

"For who? Him? His wife?"

The woman looked at her with wide eyes. "How did you know?"

Megan hadn't. She'd taken a wild guess. What kind

of man was being blackmailed by a sex shop? He had to have something to hide from someone. And he had to have the money to pay. "So what are they? Videos?"

Samantha didn't answer, but she didn't have to.

"Videos of him with another woman?"

Samantha looked away.

"Videos of him with you?"

Her focus shot back to Megan's face.

"That's it. You set him up."

"Not on purpose. I didn't know Julianne was recording everything. She had a whole business, she and her Valducci partners. But even though she used me to set them up, she wouldn't cut me in on it. But Evan—"

"Evan Blankenship?" Megan couldn't believe her ears. Had Evan killed people in order to protect his job as a small town mayor? No. Of course not. That wasn't it at all. He did it to protect his marriage to Harris the heiress. A marriage that probably came with a prenup.

"He promised me that if I destroyed the videos of us, he'd let me have the rest. If I destroy the computer, I'll have nothing."

"Maybe the plan didn't go awry. Maybe that's what he intended all along."

The blonde shook her head.

Megan could tell she was getting to the woman. She pressed on. "Maybe he always intended to hang you out to dry for setting him up in the first place. Or worse, maybe he thinks you're as much of a liability as Derek and Doug."

Samantha leaned toward her, knuckles white on the

gun's handle. "You have to get into the computer. You have to copy a video. At least one."

"And you have to bring me my son."

"I can kill you. I can shoot you right now." She brought the gun up to Megan's head and pressed the barrel against her temple.

Megan's pulse thrummed in her ears. The metal was cold against her skin. Her hands felt clammy. She thought of the crack of gunfire that had come from the alley. The shape of a person splayed on the ground. Too large for Connor. Was it Ty? "Go ahead, shoot me. Then you'll be next. And he is going to be the only one who gets out of this."

"I'm not going to let him do that to me." The woman reached for her cell phone and punched Redial.

Raising her arm, Megan spun in the desk chair. Her elbow struck Samantha Vickery square in the face.

She staggered backward. The gun and the cell phone skittered to the floor.

The sound of a ring came from outside the window. "Yes?" a male voice barked from the phone.

Megan hit the woman again, putting her full weight behind the blow.

Samantha's head jolted back and she fell on her hands and knees. She propped herself up for a moment, stunned, then started sweeping the floor with her hands.

The gun.

Megan scanned the floor. There it was. Under the corner of the desk. She dove for it. Her hand closed over the cold metal. She fitted it into her palms and turned around.

"Kill the boy."

Megan leveled the gun on her, but her finger wouldn't pull the trigger.

"Evan? Kill the boy. Now," Samantha screamed into the phone.

Outside, another gunshot split the air.

TY LOWERED HIS GUN AND SLUMPED against the Dumpster. He eyed the body of Lake Hubbard's mayor, shot and bleeding in the dirty alley behind a sex shop. Evan Blankenship. Ty hadn't seen it, not for a second. All the time he'd spent being jealous that Evan was offering Megan support, getting her job back for her, all of it—and he was actually behind this whole thing.

A woman's voice squawked over Blankenship's phone.

Megan was still inside. She needed his help. He needed to get in there.

He gritted his teeth and tried to push to his feet. Pain racheted through him. He couldn't breathe. He couldn't move. He'd promised her. He'd promised. And yet he was no help at all.

He couldn't believe he'd let the bastard sneak up on him. Let him shoot. But he hadn't seen him. Not at all. One minute the alley was empty, the next...

Ty squinted into the darkness along the wrought iron fence. All the legends of the old lake mansions flitted through his mind. The most legendary, of course, being Harris House.

Lights flashed in the sky, red and blue. A squad car skidded into the mouth of the alley, another behind it.

Ed and Trevor jumped out of the driver's doors, guns drawn.

"Over here," Ty yelled as best he could. "I'm injured. The mayor is likely dead. There are two women in the shop. Megan and Samantha Vickery. Vickery has a gun. Hurry." He gasped for breath, each wheeze brought with it a white-hot pain that made him feel as if he was about to pass out. "And Harris House. There's a tunnel over there, by the fence. Connor Burke is inside."

The back door of the shop flew open. An alarm screamed through the alley. And standing with her hands up, her cheek red and bleeding and her hair a wild tangle, was the sweetest sight Ty had ever seen. "Megan."

MEGAN BARELY LOOKED AT EVAN Blankenship lying face down on the ground in his expensive overcoat. She raced to Ty's side and fell to her knees beside him. "Are you okay?"

"I'm fine. Where's Vickery?"

"Inside." She glanced up at the two patrol cops she'd met when she'd set off the alarm at Keating. "I put handcuffs on her."

Ty's laugh disintegrated into coughing.

She leaned over him. For the first time, she noticed his coat was soaked with blood. "You're not okay. You've been shot." It had been Ty she'd seen on the ground. She glanced at the dark form of Evan Blankenship. "And you shot Evan."

"It was the least I could do after he shot me."

She glanced over the area. It was just Ty and Evan. No sign of her son. "And Connor?"

"In the tunnel." He exchanged a look with Trevor. "You'll find him in there. I know you will."

Megan was almost afraid to ask. "Find him?"

More lights flashed into the alley. Detective Baker and another uniformed patrolman rushed up to them.

Ed motioned to the new officer. "Inside. With me." Guns drawn, they entered the shop.

Ty glanced from Megan to Baker. "The bootlegger tunnels. One of them opens right here, by the fence. It's how Blankenship got the drop on me."

Detective Baker nodded to Trevor. They started in the direction Ty had indicated.

Megan scrambled to her feet. She looked back at Ty. He was bleeding. He might die.

"Go," he said.

Tears filled her eyes.

"There are plenty of cops here now. I'll be fine. Your son needs you."

She nodded. After all he'd given her, he was still watching out for her. She didn't know how she'd let fear rule over her all these years. After tonight, it wouldn't rule over her again.

She ran after Trevor and Detective Baker.

Normally she probably wouldn't have been able to find the gate. Especially not at night. It blended in with the rest of the fence. But it was unlocked and partly open, as if Blankenship had been in a hurry and hadn't bothered to secure it. Or maybe he'd intended to go right back.

Trevor pulled out his flashlight, shining it over the grounds. A garden shed stood near the fence.

"Stand back, Ms. Garvey," the detective said in a low voice. "Keep behind us."

The cops pulled out their guns. Trevor opened the door, shining the light inside.

Even from a distance, Megan could see the shed was empty except for a staircase reaching down deep into the ground.

"Stay here," the detective ordered. "I mean it." Guns at the ready, the two police officers descended the stairs.

Megan inched toward the shed. Was her baby down there? Was he alive? She couldn't breathe. Dry sobs wracked her chest, and still the air wouldn't come.

Please let him be alive. Let him be okay.

She didn't know how much time had passed when she heard footsteps coming up the concrete stairs. She saw detective Baker first. He cradled a little body in his arms.

Her knees wobbled and failed. She sagged to the ground.

Baker stepped out of the shed and knelt down beside her. "Here you go, buddy. Here she is."

Connor nearly flew into her arms. Megan held him close, tears rushing down her face. She held him and kissed him and swore she would never again let him go.

WHEN MEGAN FINALLY RETURNED to the alley with Connor in her arms, Ty had already been taken to the hospital. Sergeant Taylor drove her and Connor there. And while Megan waited for Ty to get out of surgery, she went over everything that had happened with Sergeant

Taylor and Detective Baker. By the time they left her in peace, she'd told the story so many times, it felt distant, as if it might have happened to someone else.

Finally Ty awakened and was given a room, and a nurse told Megan that she could see him. She led Connor into the room by one hand. He clutched two action figures in the other, a gift from Sergeant Taylor's older boys who no longer played with them.

Her first glimpse of Ty made her want to cry. He was leaning back against his pillow. His face was so pale, it made her chest ache.

He opened his eyes, and a smile curved the corners of his lips. "Good to see you, Connor, my man."

"Hi, Ty." He held up his toys. "I got a Spiderman and an Indiana Jones."

"Cool." Ty gave Megan a wink.

Connor scampered to the window sill on the other side of Ty's bed and made his action figures climb over a potted plant bearing a card from the police department.

Megan stepped close to Ty's bed. She reached out and took his fingers in hers, careful not to tangle the IV tube snaking into the back of his hand. "How are you doing?"

"I've been better." He gave her a weak smile. "I promised I'd help you, and here I'm the one who needed the help."

"Connor is safe because of you. I'm safe." She squeezed his hand. Ty had to be okay. He had to be. "We wouldn't be here if it weren't for you."

He let out a sigh. "It didn't go as smoothly as I'd hoped."

"Really? You weren't planning to get shot?"

He reached up and touched the bruise and scuff on her cheek. "I wasn't the only one who got hurt."

"This is nothing."

"You were incredible the way you handled Vickery. Leo says she's been talking all night."

"That's good."

"She used to work for Julianne, whose maiden name happens to be Valducci. And as it turns out, they did provide in-home massage and a lot of other things—or at least Vickery did. There's video to prove it. And the home where she took her clients was owned by Marco Valducci's brother. It was the mansion across from Harris House."

"Where we found Doug's body," she whispered, as she looked over her shoulder at Connor, still playing at the windowsill.

Ty's head moved in a slight nod.

She wasn't sure what she felt about Doug's death. It hadn't yet sunk in, probably. She could guess that he saw the scam as an easy way to help out his old pal Evan and get the money he needed to pay off the Valduccis, although how he could have involved their son in all that, she couldn't fathom. Somehow she would have to explain it all to Connor.

"So were they fur lined?"

She shook her head, not following.

"The handcuffs you put on her. Were they fur lined? I've been wondering ever since the alley."

She couldn't help but smile. "Fake fur. Leopard print."

"You've got style, Ms. Garvey."

"Thanks." A laugh bubbled in her chest. He always had that power. The ability to bring her out of herself, keep her from obsessing too much over her own thoughts. The only other person who could make her forget herself like that was Connor.

And now she had them both. Safe.

But as much as she loved bantering with Ty, that wasn't why she'd needed to see him. She needed to tell him what she thought, how she was feeling. She'd wasted so much time being afraid, she didn't want another moment to pass before she moved on. Before she took the leap. "We need to talk."

He raised his brows. "Isn't that what we've been doing?"

"You know what I mean. Really talk."

He nodded. "Okay. I love—"

She pressed her fingertips to his lips. "No. Me first."

"Okay," he said, the word muffled against her fingers.

Now that he was looking at her, waiting for her to speak, she couldn't find a word in her head. She took a deep breath and let it out slowly. "I was so afraid."

He waited for her to follow up, but the words stuck in her throat. Finally he nodded, encouraging. "Afraid?"

Tears filled her eyes, making the hospital room, Ty and his bed a wavy mosaic of color. It had been so easy in the waiting room when she'd been rehearsing her speech in her head. Now all she could think about was how much she felt for him, how relieved she was that things were over, how eager she was to move on.

She scooped in a deep breath and plunged. "I was afraid of being hurt. Of not seeing something I should until it was too late. Not making the right choices. I convinced myself if I could make it alone, I wouldn't have to worry about any of those things." The words rushed out in a jumbled torrent. They didn't make a lot of sense, but she hoped that after their recent discussions, he'd be able to follow.

"You *can* make it alone."

She shook her head. She wasn't saying this right. It wasn't coming out right at all. "That's not the point, Ty. I don't *want* to make it alone. I want you with me."

"I'm not going to die, Megan."

A laugh bubbled in her chest. "You'd better not, Ty, because I love you."

He pulled her hand, bringing her toward him.

She lowered her mouth to his and gave him a gentle kiss. Tears broke free and rolled down her cheeks. "I always have loved you, you know. Since we were kids. I just never let myself risk…" She shook her head.

"You've been through hell, Megan. With your parents. With me leaving you back then. With Doug. And now? Now you need time to heal."

Heal. Yes, she did. "We both need time to heal. I just want to know, if it's okay with you, could we do our healing together?"

"Yeah. Of course. I'd like that." He cupped a hand around her neck and brought her lips back to his.

This time the kiss wasn't gentle but needy, passionate. Warmth filled her to overflowing and her knees felt weak. She leaned a hip on the bed to keep her balance. And when the kiss ended and she looked into his eyes, she felt stronger already. As if the healing had indeed begun.

Epilogue

The sky was clear on Christmas morning, and the sunlight bounced off blinding-white snow and streamed in through Megan's apartment windows, bright enough to make Ty want to keep his sunglasses on, even inside. Not that he would. He didn't want to miss one moment of the little boy Christmas action, after all. He pulled off his coat and shades and squinted against the glare. "Hey there, little man! Merry Christmas."

"Santa came. Look, Ty!" Connor bounced up and down on his toes and pointed to the mound of wrapped packages wedged under the tree.

Ty exchanged a big grin with Megan. "You bet Santa came, buddy. I wonder what he brought."

Connor turned his big eyes on Megan. "Can I see, mommy?"

"As soon as I get Ty some coffee, honey." She beamed at him. "Merry Christmas."

"Merry Christmas," he answered. He wrapped his arm around her shoulders and kissed her.

Her lips tasted like donuts and coffee, and suddenly he was very hungry. But not for food. He couldn't believe three weeks had passed since they'd gotten Connor back safe and sound. The time had streamed by in a blur. His release from the hospital. Doug's funeral. Samantha Vickery talking to anyone who would listen. His suspension from the police department had been lifted, and once he had recovered from the gunshot wound, he would return to the job he loved. Megan had been charged with a misdemeanor for breaking into Keating Security, but even that charge would probably be dropped.

He'd spent every day with Megan and Connor, every hour he possibly could, and they were healing, both of them. But even though everything had gone better than he'd ever dreamed, he worried he might be rushing things now.

Megan beamed at him. "I'll be right back." She walked into the kitchen, him enjoying the view. When she rounded the corner, he glanced back in the direction of the construction paper fireplace he and Connor had made and taped to the wall. Two stockings hung from the pretend mantle, one for Connor and one for Megan.

God, he was nervous.

Out of all the things he'd tried to give Megan, this was the one he was most worried about. He had to be crazy, risking what they'd shared in the past weeks. But he had to know. Megan had never allowed herself to need him, never allowed him to give her anything. She'd moved on in the past weeks, but he had to wonder if she'd moved on enough to accept this.

Still, he had to know. He'd been in love with Megan Garvey for most of his life. He had to know, really know, if she was in love with him enough to put the past behind.

Megan handed him a mug of coffee and set a plate of crullers on the table in front of the couch. "For a special treat." She smiled, and for a moment, he found it hard to breathe.

She turned a smile on her son. "Connor? Do you want to start or should—"

"I want to!" The little dude plopped to his knees amid the boxes and grabbed a big one with a blue bow and green and red paper. "This is for you, Mommy."

"Thank you, sweetie. But I meant, would you like to start opening your presents?"

"You open this." He shoved the box at Megan.

Ty tried to hide his smile. He couldn't wait to see how this went.

Megan carefully plucked off the bow and stuck it on her son's head.

"I'm a present," he said.

"You sure are." She exchanged smiles with Ty and tore the paper. The next glance she gave him was a little on the confused side. She opened a cardboard flap and pulled out a pair of fuzzy dog-paw slippers. "Wow."

"They're for you, Mommy."

"Oh, I see. Thank you." She kissed the top of his head.

"Ty helped me pick those. He said they would make you look pretty."

"He did, did he?"

Ty struggled to hold in his chuckle. He'd started to

heal, all right, but his chest still hurt like hell. "Try them on."

She gave him an exaggerated frown.

"Yeah, Mommy. Try them on."

She slipped her feet into the paws.

"Fashion show." Ty tilted his index finger downward and made a twirling motion.

She stepped out among the gifts and started strutting like a fashion model. By the time she was finished, Ty's sides ached to high heaven, and Connor was bouncing off the wall with excited energy. "Me next," he said.

Megan smiled. "Yes, you next. I need some time to absorb these."

Connor made short work of his gifts. Soon he was sitting on the floor amid crumpled paper, his hair festooned with bows. He fitted together his new Legos, his little tongue poking between his lips, oblivious to everything around him.

"I guess it's our turn," Megan said.

A jitter seized Ty's stomach. Now that the time had come, he wasn't sure he could go through with it. If she didn't accept it, what then? The past weeks had been all he could possibly dream of, all he could want. If this didn't go well, would it all be over, like last time? Was he pushing too hard?

"Here's one." Megan handed him a shirt box.

He let out a breath, grateful for the delay, yet growing more anxious at the same time. He stuck the bow on Connor's back and ripped the paper. He opened the box, revealing a Milwaukee Brewer's jersey with his name on the back. "I've always wanted one of these. Thanks."

Gifts for Megan revealed a series of novels she wanted, a new yoga mat, a jewelry box and a green blouse to make up for that teddy Ty still saw her wearing in his dreams. Someday. Ty hauled in a Packer jersey for football season wear and a watch.

"One last thing," Ty said, managing to force the words past the knot in his throat. "You two didn't check your stockings."

Connor perked up from his toys. "We don't have a real fireplace and real stockings."

"The stockings sure look real to me." Ty stepped to the paper fireplace they'd stuck to the wall and motioned the two of them to follow. "Check it out. Santa can make all kinds of wishes real. Don't you know that?"

"It is real," Connor said on an awed breath. He grabbed the small stocking with his name on it and unstuck it from the paper fireplace. He peered inside and pulled out a Hot Wheels car and a bag of Teddy Grahams. He plopped back on the floor among his toys. "You too, Mommy. Look."

Megan gave Ty a guarded smile. She stepped to the paper fireplace and detached the stocking. Ty held his breath as she shoved her hand inside.

She pulled out an oblong box. Giving him a little smile, she opened it. "Oh my God. Is this the same one?" She reached in the box, pulled out the diamond bracelet and held it aloft.

"I was wondering if the timing was better this time."

She smiled, her green eyes twinkling. "Help me put it on."

He took the bracelet and strung it around her wrist. His big fingers were so clumsy, it took him four tries to secure the clasp.

She stretched out her arm. The diamonds sparkled against her skin. "It's beautiful."

He realized he was still holding his breath. He let it out and inhaled into hungry lungs. "I wanted it to be a diamond ring, but I thought that might be pushing things a bit."

He thought she might agree with him on that one, but she just smiled as if she knew a secret he would soon find out.

"Maybe you'll find one of those in your stocking next Christmas."

"I'll put it on my list for Santa."

He kissed her again. "I doubt I'll last until Christmas."

"Well, maybe Santa will fill my stocking other days of the year." She gave him a teasing smile and raised her eyebrows.

Realizing how quiet it was in the apartment, he glanced around. Connor lay in the jumble of wrapping and ribbon and toys, face down and fast asleep. "He's had a big morning."

Megan followed his gaze and smiled. "It's time for his nap, anyway. I should carry him to bed." She moved to get up.

Ty took her hand. "Why not leave him with his toys? What will it hurt? Besides, I was thinking I'd give you my other present."

"There's more?"

"Yep. One present for you and one for me."

"Is that so?"

He kissed her again. He was so relieved Megan had accepted the bracelet. For him it washed away the past, but it was more than just that. It cleared the way for the future. It said she wouldn't fight needing him. And that was good, since he liked feeling needed…and he couldn't help needing her.

And she would get that ring. Sooner rather than later. Spending his life with Megan would be the best present he could imagine. Living each day with her and Connor would give him the ultimate joy.

Letting his hand trail down to her blouse, he freed the first button. "We might want to unwrap these last two presents in the bedroom."

* * * * *

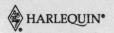 HARLEQUIN®

INTRIGUE®

COMING NEXT MONTH

Available November 9, 2010

#1239 BODY ARMOR
Bodyguard of the Month
Alana Matthews

#1240 HIGH-CALIBER CHRISTMAS
Whitehorse, Montana: Winchester Ranch Reloaded
B.J. Daniels

#1241 COLBY BRASS
Colby Agency: Christmas Miracles
Debra Webb

#1242 SAVIOR IN THE SADDLE
Texas Maternity: Labor and Delivery
Delores Fossen

#1243 THE PEDIATRICIAN'S PERSONAL PROTECTOR
The Delancey Dynasty
Mallory Kane

#1244 HOSTAGE TO THUNDER HORSE
Elle James

LARGER-PRINT BOOKS!

GET 2 FREE LARGER-PRINT NOVELS

PLUS 2 FREE GIFTS!

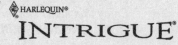

HARLEQUIN®

INTRIGUE®

Breathtaking Romantic Suspense

YES! Please send me 2 FREE LARGER-PRINT Harlequin Intrigue® novels and my 2 FREE gifts (gifts are worth about $10). After receiving them, if I don't wish to receive any more books, I can return the shipping statement marked "cancel." If I don't cancel, I will receive 6 brand-new novels every month and be billed just $4.99 per book in the U.S. or $5.74 per book in Canada. That's a saving of at least 13% off the cover price! It's quite a bargain! Shipping and handling is just 50¢ per book.* I understand that accepting the 2 free books and gifts places me under no obligation to buy anything. I can always return a shipment and cancel at any time. Even if I never buy another book from Harlequin, the two free books and gifts are mine to keep forever.

199/399 HDN E5MS

Name _____ (PLEASE PRINT) _____

Address _____ Apt. # _____

City _____ State/Prov. _____ Zip/Postal Code _____

Signature (if under 18, a parent or guardian must sign)

Mail to the Harlequin Reader Service:
IN U.S.A.: P.O. Box 1867, Buffalo, NY 14240-1867
IN CANADA: P.O. Box 609, Fort Erie, Ontario L2A 5X3

Not valid for current subscribers to Harlequin Intrigue Larger-Print books.

Are you a subscriber to Harlequin Intrigue books and want to receive the larger-print edition? Call 1-800-873-8635 today!

* Terms and prices subject to change without notice. Prices do not include applicable taxes. N.Y. residents add applicable sales tax. Canadian residents will be charged applicable provincial taxes and GST. Offer not valid in Quebec. This offer is limited to one order per household. All orders subject to approval. Credit or debit balances in a customer's account(s) may be offset by any other outstanding balance owed by or to the customer. Please allow 4 to 6 weeks for delivery. Offer available while quantities last.

Your Privacy: Harlequin Books is committed to protecting your privacy. Our Privacy Policy is available online at www.eHarlequin.com or upon request from the Reader Service. From time to time we make our lists of customers available to reputable third parties who may have a product or service of interest to you. If you would prefer we not share your name and address, please check here. ☐

Help us get it right—We strive for accurate, respectful and relevant communications. To clarify or modify your communication preferences, visit us at www.ReaderService.com/consumerschoice.

HILP10R

**The mission trip to Mexico was supposed to be an
adventure. But the thrill turns sour when Jenna Dougherty
and her roommate Magdalena are kidnapped.**

"It's okay. I'm here to help." The voice was as deep as the
darkness, but Jenna Dougherty didn't believe the lie. She
could do nothing but lie still as hands slid down her arms,
felt the rope around her wrists.

"I'm going to use a knife to cut you free, Jenna. Hold
still."

The cold blade of a knife pressed close to her head before
her gag fell away.

"I—" she started, but her mouth was dry, and she could
do nothing but suck in air.

"Shhh. Whatever needs to be said can be said when
we're out of here." Nick spoke quietly, his hand gentle on
her cheek. There and gone as he sliced through the ropes on
her wrists and ankles.

He pulled her upright. "Come on. We may be on
borrowed time."

"I can't leave my friend," Jenna rasped out.

"There's no one here. Just us."

"She has to be here." Jenna took a step away.

"There's no one here. Let's go before that changes."

"It's dark. Maybe if we find a light…"

"What did you say?"

"We need to turn on the light. I can't leave until I know that—"

"What can you see, Jenna?"

"Nothing."

"No shadows? No light?"

"No."

"It's broad daylight. There's light spilling in from the window I climbed in through. You can't see it?"

She went cold at his words.

"I can't see anything."

"You've got a nasty bruise on your forehead. Maybe that has something to do with it." His fingers traced the tender flesh on her forehead.

"It doesn't matter *how* it happened. I'm blind!"

Can Nick help Jenna find her friend or will chasing this trail have Jenna running blindly again into danger?

Find out in RUNNING BLIND, available in November 2010 only from Love Inspired Suspense.